Constable Petra Jensen
Greenland Missing Persons
Omnibus Edition #1
Books 1-3

Christoffer Petersen

CONSTABLE PETRA JENSEN 1-3

Constable Petra Jensen
Greenland Missing Persons
Omnibus Edition 1, books 1-3

Copyright © Christoffer Petersen 2023

Christoffer Petersen has asserted his right under the Copyright, Designs and Patents Act 1988 to be identified as the author of this work.

This book is a work of fiction. The names, characters, places and incidents are products of the writer's imagination or have been used fictitiously and are not to be construed as real. Any resemblance to persons, living or dead, actual events or organisations is entirely coincidental.

All rights reserved. No part of this publication may be reproduced, stored in a retrieval system, or transmitted, in any form or by any means, without the prior permission in writing of the publisher, nor be otherwise circulated in any form of binding or cover other than that in which it is published and without a similar condition including this condition being imposed on the subsequent purchaser.

ISBN: 9798396619302

CHRISTOFFER PETERSEN

Praise for Christoffer Petersen's Greenland books

"The Arctic chill has never been as seductive as in Christoffer Petersen's books."
– **Lilja Sigurðardóttir**, author of *Snare*, *Trap* and *Cage*

"You might want to put your warmest coat on. Christoffer Petersen writes chilling thrillers in harsh, isolated environments. Too dark for some. Too cold for everyone."
– **Óskar Guðmundsson**, author of *Hilma* and *Blood Angel*

"Sharp and authentic – Greenland will haunt you after this."
– **Quentin Bates**, author of the *Gunnhildur Crime Mysteries*

"Petersen brings Greenland to life, and death to Greenland. A tale of extraordinary people in an extraordinary setting. I was gripped from the first grave."
– **Michael Ridpath**, author of the *Magnus Iceland Mysteries*

"Christoffer Petersen is a terrific writer, and his books bring Greenland compellingly to life in all its

CONSTABLE PETRA JENSEN 1-3

harsh beauty."
– **Kevin Wignall**, author of *A Death in Sweden*

"Chilling crimes, stark settings, and the remote Arctic brought to life. Petersen's depth of knowledge make his thrillers unmissable for any lover of extremes."
– **J.F. Penn**, author of the *Arkane* series

"Petra Jensen is an intriguing character, and the Greenland setting makes for compelling reading."
– **Margaret Kirk**, author of the *DI Lukas Mahler* series

"No one writes Arctic Noir like Petersen! Bleak landscapes, action-packed thrillers, fabulous cultural insight and a cast of intriguing characters That simply leave you wanting more!"
– **Dr Noir**, organiser of *Newcastle Noir*

"Christoffer Petersen is the master of Arctic crime."
– **William Burton McCormick**, author of *KGB Banker* and *Lenin's Harem*

CHRISTOFFER PETERSEN

Introduction to the Omnibus Editions

Ever since *We Shall Be Monsters*, book three in the Greenland Crime series, I have wanted to make amends to Petra. No matter how I try to justify what happened to her in that book, for the sake of the series, I still feel bad. *We Shall Be Monsters* is a dark book. Some readers like it, others–including many of the same readers–prefer the *Greenland Missing Persons* series of novellas, novels, and short stories. These books are lighter, faster, quirkier, and yet not quite cosy mysteries. With each book in this series, I try to make it up to Petra. Yes, she's real to me. And *yes*, I still feel guilty.

However, in an attempt to *move on*, I am very excited to present to you, dear reader, the omnibus editions of the *Greenland Missing Persons* series. In the same way that Constable David Maratse's novellas helped define him, these books are true to Petra's character at the very beginning of her career, and include heaps of wonderful insight into Greenland, the people, culture, and traditions, as experienced by me during the seven incredible years I lived there. I hope you will join me and travel to Greenland through the pages of these omnibus editions, and I hope your interest in Greenland is sufficiently piqued.

CONSTABLE PETRA JENSEN 1-3

If it is, then I have done my job.

The rest, as Luui would say, is *Magic!*

Chris
October 2021
Denmark

CHRISTOFFER PETERSEN

Glossary of Greenlandic Words
used in the *Greenland Missing Persons* series

aap – yes
ana – grandmother
anaana – mother
angakkoq – shaman
ata – grandfather
ataata – father
imaqa – maybe
naamik – no
kaffemik – celebration/party
kamikker/kamiks – sealskin boots
mattak – whale skin and blubber delicacy
qajaq – kayak
qujanaq – thank you [roo-yah]
tuttu – reindeer
ukaleq – Arctic hare

tulugaq – raven

CONSTABLE PETRA JENSEN 1-3

The Boy with the Narwhal Tooth

Greenland Missing Persons #1

CHRISTOFFER PETERSEN

Introduction

There are two questions about my writing that scare me the most. The first is *how many books have you written?* I've never been good at mathematics, but it should be an easy answer, a straightforward sum – just add them all up. But I've been exploring Greenland through my stories for a little while now, through novels, novellas, short stories, and collections, even poems and essays. So much so, my stock answer is usually twenty novels and twenty-five novellas, but I'm not sure about that anymore.

The second question is equally frightening, perhaps even more so. *What order should I read your books in?* Or *which book should I start with?* I have prequels and sequels and stand-alones. Some of my books are set in the past; others are set far into the future. They are nearly all linked through one character or another. I write these stories as I think about them. There is no grand plan, but perhaps a few rules of thumb. But let's keep it simple, and start with the book you have in your hands or on your eReader, phone, or tablet.

The Boy with the Narwhal Tooth is set at the very beginning of Petra Jensen's career as a police constable in Greenland. It is by no means a typical career, nor are these stories to be confused with the real police work in Greenland. They are *inspired* by what I witnessed and experienced, and then injected with a heavy dose of myth, culture, tradition and drama. Regardless of the accuracy of the details, *The Boy with the Narwhal Tooth* is story #1 in Petra's police career.

I call her Petra, but if you've read any of my other stories, and if you've met Constable David Maratse, you'll know he calls her *Piitalaat*.

These are her stories

Let's begin with this one.

Chris
June 2020
Denmark

1

It's a cliché, I know, but it really did start with a telephone, an empty desk and a generous new police commissioner, giving my career a gentle shove in the right direction. Fresh out of Greenland's Police Academy, my boots were still buffed, and my jacket had that factory smell of wax and freshly stitched seams. During training, I had become expert at flattening my hair, tugging it into a tight ponytail that I had learned to flick out of the way of opportunists' hands, when sparring in the gym. I had also learned to tone down my perfume and scented shampoos, allowing myself just enough scent to arouse interest from my single colleagues – *I graduated from a police academy, not a nunnery.* And, aside from my utility belt swagger – the *only* weight I wanted on my hips –I had learned that while a clean sidearm could be seen across a crowded room, a speck of dust or fluff in the trigger guard could be seen a mile away. In short, I was ready for duty, ready to be hazed, to give as good as I got, to respect experience, but also to make the most of my twenty-three years, and to put my orphan past behind me. I had, figuratively and physically, big boots to fill, measured by my own aspirations and a less than comfortable past.

Unfortunately, during my first weeks on the

job, I did little more than get in the way.

"Training is over, Jensen."

I must have heard that little gem about a thousand times in the first week, and a thousand more in the second. One man in particular made a point of working it into each and every situation imaginable, from pulling out of the parking lot, to making coffee. Sergeant Kiiu "George" Duneq was always there. I could never shake him. To be fair, he was partly responsible for making sure I learned the ropes, that I transitioned from newly graduated police constable, to a useful working part of what he seemed to think was a well-oiled machine. Sergeant Duneq was my supervisor, and I spent far too much time hating him when I should have been paying more attention to a briefing. He seemed to enjoy it when I stumbled, adding comments about my physical appearance – *too pretty for police work*. I was, I will admit, far prettier than him, but that was all I had on him. His girth, the way his utility belt had extra holes in it, belly hanging over the buckle, like his jowls melting over the collar of his dirty shirt – these things were the only things I could comment on, and only when I was alone, or sometimes with Constable Atii Napa, when we had a night off together.

"Fluff on his trigger guard," she said, shouting over the beat and thump of *Mattak*, Nuuk's most popular nightclub. "I saw it, I tell you."

"But no one else did, I bet you," I shouted back.

Even after a few drinks, blinking in the purple blue swathes of disco lights, I could still picture Sergeant Duneq's greasy black hair, and the tiny flakes of skin clinging to his bushy eyebrows. I flinched when Atii dropped her glass, looking at the door expecting to see him there, telling me with a fleshy grin that *training was over*.

He didn't have to tell *me* that, but Atii could have used a few reminders, I thought, as I slipped out of the booth and tugged her into my arms. When we graduated together, the new police commissioner addressed our class of six police graduates, reminding us to look out for each other. He told us we were never off duty, and if a colleague needed help, we were to give it, unquestioningly, but I would have done it anyway. So I helped Atii home that night, undressed her, wiped her sweaty brow, tucked her into her large double bed, and crawled in beside her. I turned her head to one side each time she rolled onto her belly, and then held her hair each time she crawled out of bed to pitch her drinks into the toilet.

I reminded myself that this was the life I had dreamed about, the career I had worked hard for. But now that my duty days and nights were spent with *Sergeant Jowls*, as I called him, and my nights off became a mix of controlled abandon and Atii's projectile vomiting, I did begin to wonder if it would ever change for the better.

Luckily for me, it did, the very next day.

2

Commissioner Lars Andersen, new to Greenland and newly arrived from Denmark, had a secret. I wasn't sure how many of my colleagues had noticed, the commissioner seemed to prefer short communiqués, and even shorter email messages. Most of my younger colleagues, digital natives such as myself, probably didn't notice, but I imagined that a few of the older hands, especially the administrative staff, would soon query the commissioner's short form communication, if they hadn't already done so. Danish was my first language, and it was one of the few things I was really good at, with English and German a close second. Greenlandic, the language of my country, however, escaped me. But the Danish that the commissioner preferred was short to the point of simplistic. It wasn't that he didn't have a flair for language; he held vigorous speeches with plenty of adjectives and anecdotes. But I had seen a pattern in his communication, and when the opportunity presented itself, I asked him about it.

That opportunity came shortly after a long sigh and a string of quiet but enthusiastic curses. I was in the outer office of the administrative wing of Nuuk Police Station, ignoring the persistent beep of a *call waiting* tone from the telephone at an empty desk at the far end, furthest from the commissioner's office. Sergeant Jowls had told me to wait while he added the finishing touches, as he called them, to his supervisory report, something he enjoyed reminding me of whenever he felt I needed what he called a *confidence boost*. The number of reminders I received seemed to increase as I gained increasing competence – and confidence – in different skills, not least when we were out on patrol, and I was driving. I smiled at the recent image of Sergeant Jowls squeezing in behind the steering wheel to show me how to drive on icy roads, as if the first two hours of the patrol didn't count.

The commissioner cursed again, louder the second time, and I heard him toss a sheaf of papers onto his desk, before he stormed out of the office, fingers gripping a bright red coffee mug.

"Constable," he said, pulling up short at the door of his office. "How long have you been there?"

"A few minutes, Sir," I said. I focused on his coffee mug, wondering if it would crack under the pressure of the commissioner's frustration.

"Long enough, I suppose."

"Yes, Sir."

The commissioner was taller than most of the police officers in Nuuk, but a little shorter than Sergeant Gaba Alatak, the bold and bald leader of the police Special Response Unit, the SRU. Atii had her sights on him already, and, in a moment of weakness, I admitted that I understood why. I caught myself daydreaming and refocused, dialling in as the commissioner asked me a question.

"You don't speak Greenlandic, do you?"

"No, Sir."

"Any reason?"

I wondered just how much to say, and how much he might have read about my past. The commissioner turned his back on me to refresh his coffee, and I took a moment. Somehow I needed to condense my early years in the Nuuk Children's Home, the years of teasing through school, and the sudden light at the end of the tunnel that came with a single room in the gymnasium Halls of Residence. It was about the same time when I discovered a love for the order and rules of grammar and a certain mixer called *Mokaï*.

"I just never learned, Sir," I said, when he turned around. "There were other things to deal with."

"Okay," he said, cradling the mug in his hands as he leaned against the sideboard. "But you know Danish?"

"Yes," I said.

"Good grade at gymnasium?"

"Yes." I blushed, and then again when I realised Atii would tease me about it forever, just like she did in gymnasium.

"Constable," the commissioner said, with a nod to his office. "If you've got nothing better to do just now, perhaps you could help me with something?"

"Of course," I said, taking a step forward.

He paused at the door, frowning at the desk in the corner of the long outer office.

"That phone has been beeping all morning. And the staff," he said, gesturing at the empty desks, "are on a course. Back after lunch. All calls have been diverted to the front desk, but they must have forgotten that one. Never mind," he said, with a nod for me to walk ahead of him. "I'm sure someone will answer it later."

"Yes, Sir," I said, sitting down on the chair in front of his desk as he slumped onto the office chair behind it.

"There's a report due," he said, setting his coffee down beside a sheaf of untidy papers. "And I just can't get my head around it. Do you think you could have a look at my notes?"

"Yes, Sir," I said, wondering what Sergeant Jowls would think when he arrived.

3

The commissioner's words were a mess. I said nothing for a full minute. He sipped his coffee and smiled when I looked up from his notes.

"You can speak freely, Constable," he said. "I won't bite."

"Sir," I said, after a short pause. "Are you dyslexic?"

"Ah, that didn't take you long, did it?" He put his coffee down, stood up, and gestured at the small sofa, coffee table and armchair by the window. "Bring the notes he said. "You might want to spread them out on the table."

I shuffled the papers into my hand, bumping past the commissioner as he asked if I took milk in my coffee.

"No, thank you," I said. I had the notes arranged in page order by the time he came back. I took a pen from my jacket to begin correcting and adjusting the opening paragraph.

"I had a rotten school life," the commissioner said, as he handed me a mug of coffee. He sat down in the armchair as I spread his notes out on the sofa. "The kids called me stupid. I'm sure you can imagine?"

"Yes, Sir," I said, thinking back to the thousands of times I had been called stupid when the words of my country failed me.

"Just arranging all those letters, it's a big puzzle. I learned to do it," he said. "I had to, but it just takes so much time. When they diagnosed me, later in my school years, I was given that time, but you can imagine, in this position, time is in limited supply."

"Yes, Sir," I said, wincing as I burnt my tongue on the coffee.

"So," he said, with a nod to his notes. "What do you think?"

"I can tidy it up, Sir," I said. "It won't take long." I put the mug down and picked up my pen, tucking an errant strand of black hair behind my ear as I leaned over the coffee table.

"You're going to do it now?"

"Yep," I said, scratching a few notes on the first page before moving on to the other.

The commissioner sat quietly for a moment, then got up to answer a call from the phone at his desk. When he was finished, so was I.

"That's fast work, Constable."

"Yes, Sir," I said. And then, without thinking, I pushed my luck a little, blurring the lines between being helpful and sucking up to the boss. "I can do it again, if you need help another time."

The words were already out there, before I bit my lip, wishing I had said nothing at all.

The commissioner smiled, and said, "I'd like that, Constable. And if we could keep it between us?"

"Of course," I said.

"It's not an issue, but I am new, after all. I need

to make an impression."

"Yes, Sir," I said, working hard to suppress a smile. "I know what you mean."

"Good," he said, with a nod to the door. "I won't keep you any longer."

I took that as my cue to leave, but he called me back just as I reached the door.

"One more thing, Constable."

"Yes?"

"Could you pick up that phone on the way out. The one that's been beeping all morning."

"Yes, Sir."

I nodded once, tucked my hair around my ear, and then walked between the workstations of the outer office, weaving between chairs and hip-high filing cabinets, before reaching the phone at the end of the room. I had to move assorted papers, stuffing them on top of more papers inside a dusty box from the copy room, before I found the telephone. I pulled out the chair, dragging it a short way on three wheels – the fourth was missing. I perched on the desk instead, lifted the receiver, and answered the call.

"I'm sorry," I said, after the first gush of words through the line. "If you could repeat that in Danish?"

"Is that *Missing Persons*?"

"Ah," I said, stumbling. "It's the administrative office. Does that help?"

"But this *is* the Missing Persons desk?"

I pressed the handset to my ear, frowning at the rush of static, like wind on the line, as I turned up the volume.

"Yes," I said. "It could be."

"I've been waiting," said the man on the other end of the line. The wind died down for a moment, helping me identify his gender.

"Yes," I said. I turned as the commissioner stepped out of his office and walked towards me. "And how can I help you?"

"I need to report a missing person."

I tugged the pen from my jacket, pinched a piece of paper from out of the box, and waited for the man to give me the details.

"And that last bit," I said, scribbling more notes beside the first few lines I had deciphered. "If you could give me that one more time?"

I wrote the telephone number down beside the address, noting that the man was ringing from the village store, and that if I called back, I should stay on the line while they fetched him.

"I'll do that," I said. "But just one thing." I caught the commissioner's eye as he sipped coffee beside me. "Just hang on, if you could," I said.

"*Aap.*"

"Right, that last bit, one more time, to make sure I got it right. How long did you say the boy has been missing?"

"Twelve months."

"It's been a long time."

"*Aap*," the man said, adding one more thing before he ended the call.

The commissioner waited as I made a few last notes.

"Dust," he said, as I looked up.

"Sir?"

"On your jacket." He put his mug down and brushed a film of dust from my sleeve.

"Thank you."

"And the call, Constable?"

"Yes," I said. I could feel the pinch of a frown just above my nose. Atii said it was cute, one of my endearing features, but I knew it was often a sign of frustration. Sometimes, more often than I liked to admit, my frowns revealed a sudden spark of interest. The commissioner recognised it at once.

"Are you going to tell me about that call, Constable?"

"Yes, Sir," I said. "But first, I have to ask, do we have a Missing Persons Desk?"

"Well," the commissioner said with a glance at the broken chair and the dusty surface of the desk. "I suppose we do now."

4

Lots of people go missing in Greenland. But reporting a missing person was usually something done locally. Often, the missing person would turn up a day or two later, caught out in bad weather, or delayed by better weather and good hunting that prolonged a trip. Delay was part of daily life in Greenland, and a few days either side of an expected arrival was often nothing more than a slight disappointment, and a good reason to make the most of a person's visit once they did arrive.

Children, lone hunters and fishermen were a different matter, especially when the weather was worse than usual, the temperatures lower, the winds stronger. The opposite was true too, when the ice broke up earlier than usual due to warm winds. People went missing in the south of Greenland, venturing into the mountains, sometimes chasing stray sheep. But all those types of *missing* were often resolved by coordinated searches, sometimes including the Danish Royal Air Force jet with its powerful cameras. The Navy and their helicopters would be brought into the search too. The results varied, of course, just like the weather and the terrain.

"But a Missing Persons *desk*," Atii said, as she bought me a guilty coffee in *Katuaq*, Greenland's

Cultural Centre, just a few convenient strides from the police station. "Having a *desk* is like calling it a department."

I had thought the very same thing. What was needed was more like a cold case department, following up on people who were missing for longer periods of time. In this case, a whole year. What this missing persons case lacked in urgency, it more than made up for with intrigue, something I found particularly appealing.

"Yes," I said, grinning at Atii from behind a tall mug of latte. She looked so much better than the last time I saw her, and yet, at the end of a long day, we both had wayward strands of hair tickling our cheeks, but Atii's clear eyes and lack of vomit was a serious improvement.

"You have a desk, Petra," she said.

"I suppose I do."

It wasn't much of a desk, and it was quickly moved out of the main office, and into a smaller, darker space tucked underneath a staircase. Sergeant Duneq arranged it, assuring the commissioner that the existing telephone line would be hooked up and routed to the new location of Greenland's Missing Persons desk. He made a point of relocating the broken chair too. But it was the desk that made all the difference.

That word again – *desk*.

Like a whole department, all to myself.

Of course, the dust I cleaned from the desk returned two-fold, together with the grit and fine sand from the soles of my colleagues' boots as they tramped up and down the staircase. Even on that very first day, just half an hour after settling me into my new *office*, Sergeant Duneq called a meeting in the small storage space at the top of the stairs. He said it was the only place he could find to meet at such short notice, now that the work schedules had to be revised to accommodate Constable Jensen's trip to Qaanaaq. My colleagues and I clumped together, leaning in and bending with the sharp angles of the roof pressing the team together. It was agreed that the next meeting would be held in the normal place – much larger and often empty – as the potential hazing of a new constable wasn't worth the discomfort. I mouthed a silent word of thanks to the older constable who suggested it, and then did my best to avoid catching the eye of Sergeant Duneq.

My desk was, of course, covered in grit and dust when I returned to it, something Sergeant Duneq noticed with more than a little glee.

"You'll have to do something about that," he said, with another meaty smile. "When you get back."

I waited for him to leave, cleaned my desk, and then pulled it a little further from the stairs, before checking my notes. Ordinarily, I learned, there would have to be more evidence to warrant an officer being sent all the way to the top of Greenland to investigate a case that was over twelve months old, especially when the local constable had been told nothing about it. But a special flight of politicians was already scheduled, in anticipation of the next general election, and the commissioner had reserved me a seat on the flight.

"If you're going to start treading on people's toes – which you will, in this position," he said, on a follow-up visit to see what had become of the desk that had been unearthed earlier that day. "Then you may as well do it in style. And," he said, lowering his voice, "you can keep an ear out for any rumblings from the politicians on board the flight."

"I don't speak Greenlandic," I said.

"And neither do I. So, no better no worse, but you've got your head screwed on right. I trust your intuition, Constable."

"Yes, Sir," I said.

He looked at his watch. "Your flight leaves tomorrow morning. Have one of the patrol cars drop you off at the airport."

I nodded, gathered my notes, and then called Atii the minute the commissioner was gone.

"Coffee," I said. "As soon as your shift's over."

5

The month of May is a perfect time to fly in Greenland. There is plenty of snow to add sharp accents and shadows to the granite peaks, and the warm sun means that you can get away with travelling light. Not that I intended to spend much time out of doors. Once I interviewed the old man in Qaanaaq, once I *humoured* him, then I imagined I would spend the rest of the time indoors, listening to the politicians canvas the residents of Qaanaaq inside the sports hall, the school's Aula, or both. The thought amused me, as did the banter between the politicians on the flight. I chatted with one of them, a slim woman called Nivi Winther. Some people said she was tipped for the top post, if her party won the election, and the seven minutes we chatted together confirmed it for me, and I was convinced she would get my vote. But when her colleagues – all of them male – drew her away to discuss more important matters than a young female police constable might fathom, I noticed something else about Nivi Winther. Behind her natural empathy, there was fire in her bones, and I realised how important it would be for her to lead my country, to give women like me a stronger voice.

"I enjoyed talking to you, Constable," she said, as she left. "I'll leave you to your work."

CONSTABLE PETRA JENSEN 1-3

I checked my notes from Nuuk to Ilulissat, took a coffee break and several rounds of *Candy Crush* on the next hop to Upernavik, and listened to music as we descended to land. And then, back in the air, once I finished staring at the vibrant browns of the exposed mountains, and the deepest of blues and brilliant white crusts of the sea ice, I took another look at my notes, scant though they were.

According to the man on the static line from Qaanaaq, a boy, Isaja Qisuk, went missing in May the previous year. He was seven years old. His birthday was May 14th which meant he would be almost eight by the time I arrived in Qaanaaq. The only other details I had, apart from the caller's contact details, included mention of a narwhal tooth.

The tooth of the narwhal comes in many sizes, a twist of creamy ivory as thick as a man's fist, or as slender as a woman's finger. They can be long, often as tall as a seven-year-old boy, or longer still – perhaps the length of one of those cheap and tiny cars that had become popular in Greenland's capital. A hunter could easily sell a narwhal tooth to a Dane for a couple of thousand Danish kroner. Or he could carve tiny pieces of it into jewellery and make even more money. They are as valuable as they are mystical, and the romantic part of me liked to think the narwhal tooth played an important part in my first missing persons case. The old man in Qaanaaq had assured me that it did.

"It's a double tooth," he'd said when we spoke. "Twisting out of the cranium. Rare and expensive."

The line had crackled beyond coherency before

I could press more information out of him, leaving me to wonder about the connection between the boy and tooth.

The whine and shudder of the undercarriage dropping into position encouraged me to finish the last dregs of my coffee, tuck my notes into my small backpack, and tighten my seatbelt. We landed a few minutes later, bumping onto Qaanaaq's gravel landing strip with a rush of wind pummelling the air brakes. I resisted the urge to clap, smiled at the politicians who couldn't help themselves, and then looked out of the window at the tiny airport building, the flat land tapering down to the sea ice, and the long hump like a beast's back that was Herbert Island, to the south and west of Qaanaaq.

I waited for the politicians to file out of the long tubular cabin of Air Greenland's Dash-7, grabbed my backpack from beneath my seat, and joined them. The local police officer, a tall young Greenlander with pale skin and blond hair called Constable Innarik Umeerinneq greeted me and took me to one side.

"I have to stay with them," he said, nodding at the politicians.

"You know why I'm here?"

"*Aap*. But you'll find nothing. I've been here for four months. No one has said a word about the boy."

"Isaja," I said.

"Yeah, I know." Umeerinneq waved to the politicians that he was ready, apologised once more, and then suggested I try and get a lift into town. "The patrol car's full of politicians," he said. "I'm sorry. I can try and send someone back for you."

"I'll manage," I said.

"It's four kilometres," Umeerinneq said, as he slipped away.

The commissioner had said I would be treading on toes, but Umeerinneq seemed more stressed than irritated. I watched him leave, tugging my backpack onto my shoulder before walking out of the airport.

I blinked in the sun, lifting my hand to shield my eyes the second I left the building. The patrol car was the second to last car to leave the gravel parking lot, disappearing in a cloud of dust, not unlike that which covered my desk back in Nuuk. I waved at a small man leaning against the passenger door of an old pickup truck. He waved back and I walked towards him.

"I know why you're here," he said in Danish, as I approached.

"Excuse me?"

"You've come about the boy."

"Are you the man I talked to on the phone? Aluusaq?"

The man chuckled, laughter lines wrinkling the skin either side of his eyes. He had the thickest grey hair I had ever seen, short, apart from an even thicker tuft, banded at the top of his head as if he was sprouting. His hands were like warm leather as he shook mine. They were the same colour as his coffee-coloured t-shirt, the hem of which hung loosely over the waistband of his jeans. The white bristles on his chin, together with his grey hair, made me think he was at least seventy, but the flash of light in his brown eyes shed years off his tiny body.

"My name is Tuukula," he said. "And I am going to be your guide."

6

Tuukula was not alone. A small girl clambered out of the passenger seat, wedging herself in the tiny space between the driver's seat and the ribbed metal wall of the cab as I got in. The door creaked open and shut, and the hiss of the suspension as I sat down pricked the skin above my nose into a wrinkle. The girl wrinkled her own nose as if she were my mirror, but when I turned to say hello, she disappeared further into the space behind Tuukula's seat, tugging the collar of her pink t-shirt up and over her nose.

"That's Luui," he said, as he got in.

"Who is she?" I asked, tilting my head to get a better look at her. The smudges of dirt on her cheeks hid the freckles beneath them, just as she hid her eyes behind the splayed fingers of her dirty hands. She had the same thick hair as Tuukula, the same intelligent eyes, and totally disarming smile which I saw, when Tuukula started the engine and jerked the pickup into gear.

"Is she your granddaughter?"

Tuukula shook his head. "My daughter," he said, grinning when he finally crunched the gearstick into reverse. "Five years old tomorrow," he said. "We're having a *kaffemik*. You're invited."

"Oh, I'm sorry," I said. "I'll be leaving this

evening on the plane."

"I don't think so," Tuukula said, shaking his head as he bumped the pickup out of the parking space and pointed the nose towards Qaanaaq. He took a pair of sunglasses from the dashboard – the aviator kind – and reached behind his seat to tickle Luui. "Ready?" he shouted, in English.

"Ready steady," she shouted back, followed by a deep breath and the word "*Go*," shouted at the top of her tiny lungs. Tuukula stomped on the gas pedal and spun the pickup out of the parking lot around the first curve, and into the straight line heading towards the village of Qaanaaq.

Four kilometres, I thought, as I reached for the seatbelt. I tried to click it into the buckle twice before giving up. I closed my eyes for a moment. The sound of the grit and gravel peppering the underside of the car, the side panels and the windscreen forced me to open them again.

"Do you think you could slow down?" I said, grabbing for the handle above the passenger door.

"*Aap*," Tuukula said, before reaching for Luui's hand, teasing her out of her hiding place and into his lap. Luui took the wheel and Tuukula gave her his sunglasses, holding on to the ends that poked a full finger-length over her ears.

"*Ukaleq*," Luui said, pointing at a blur of white fur racing across the road ahead of us. Tuukula slammed on the brakes and I braced my hand on the dashboard as Luui slewed the pickup to a stop. The dust cloud enveloped us, as father and daughter stared through the window. Luui lifted the sunglasses from her head, looked at me and then stabbed a tiny finger against the glass. "Ukaleq."

"Yes," I said, relieved that we had stopped. "An Arctic hare."

"And ptarmigan," Tuukula said, pointing further up the mountainside at a flush of white feathers.

"Yes. I see them."

He turned the engine off. Luui continued to drive, adding motor noises of her own, as her father shifted in his seat to look at me.

"I told Aluusaq not to call you. But he is getting old. He wants to find Isaja before he dies." Tuukula bobbed his head as if he was weighing the decision in his mind before answering the old man. "I told him I would help him, if that's what he wanted, but that it would be difficult. It would be hard on him. You understand?"

"Maybe," I said.

"I told him that maybe Isaja doesn't want to be found. And if he did, then maybe Aluusaq wouldn't like what he had to tell him. But Aluusaq feels very bad. So, you are here, and I am here to guide you."

"I don't understand," I said. "You're going to guide me?"

"*Aap.*"

"Where to?"

"To find Isaja."

"Then you know where he is?"

Tuukula shook his head. "*Naamik.*"

Maybe it was the long flight, the take-offs and the landings, to which I could add the madcap race along the gravel road to Qaanaaq, but the puzzle of Isaja's disappearance was now murkier than ever.

"But if you can find him," I said. "Why haven't you looked before?"

Tuukula frowned as he looked at me. "Because he didn't want to be found."

"I don't understand."

"We'll talk later," he said, brushing Luui's hair flat against her head before kissing her cheeks. "Ready?" he whispered, reaching for the key in the ignition.

"Steady," she said.

I gripped the handle above the door and jammed my feet on either side of the footwell.

"*Go*," Luui shouted, and we launched down the gravel road.

7

The dust settled in smoky clouds around the pickup when Tuukula parked outside a small wooden cabin close to the sea ice. Luui took my hand, tugging me over the gearstick and out of the driver's door as her father held it open. I clambered out of the pickup and onto the gravel road, reaching inside the cab for my backpack as Luui made cartoon cartwheels with her stumpy legs, jerking my fingers impatiently and not letting go.

"I'm coming," I said, slipping my backpack over my shoulder as I followed Luui to the front door of the cabin.

There was more dust inside; the musty air sparkled with it. Luui tugged me across the floor and parked me in a padded armchair. The wooden arms were visible at the ends where idle fingers had tugged and teased at old upholstery. Luui chattered away in the Qaanaaq dialect, wholly unconcerned whether or not I answered, she was too busy arranging her meagre selection of toys, mostly plastic horses of various sizes, placing them on my knees, my thighs and in the folds of my jacket hanging over my lap. Tuukula grinned from the doorway to the tiny kitchen off the main room. I heard the *dunk dunk* of water bubbling out of a plastic jerry can as he prepared tea.

"Will we see Aluusaq soon?" I asked, brushing at the dirt on Luui's cheek as she crawled into my lap.

"Tomorrow," Tuukula said.

"About that," I said. "I don't think you heard me earlier."

"I heard you."

"Then perhaps you misunderstood." I lowered my voice as Tuukula appeared in the doorway. "I leave on the same plane later tonight – together with the politicians."

"*Naamik*," he said.

"Why not?"

"Because you have come all this way."

"Yes."

"But there is further to go."

"To find Isaja?"

"*Aap*." Tuukula ducked back into the kitchen as the kettle boiled. He returned with an enamel mug, chipped around the rim, and steaming with the pungent aroma of orange and winter spices. "Christmas tea," he said, pressing the mug into my hands. "I drink it all year round."

I nodded my thanks, holding the mug out of the way as Luui curled up on her side, tucking her knees to her chest and sticking a grubby thumb between wet lips.

"She's tired," Tuukula said.

"I can see that."

"She was up early, waiting for you."

"Why?"

"Because Aluusaq told her they were sending a policeman from Nuuk."

"Police *officer*," I said.

"*Aap*." Tuukula reached down to part Luui's hair with gnarled fingers. "She's excited about finding her brother."

"Isaja is her brother?"

Tuukula nodded. "Her big brother. She remembers him, asks about him all the time."

I felt the pinch of my frown and let it sit there as I processed the new information. Tuukula chuckled, and said, "I am not Isaja's father."

"But you are Luui's?"

"I am."

"Then who is Isaja's father? Aluusaq?"

"He is Isaja's grandfather. His *ata*."

Tuukula brushed the dust from the cover of a cushion before sitting down in the threadbare chair opposite me. The air sparkled between us, and I turned to look out of the sea-crusted panes of glass, just as a gaggle of small boys tumbled past with a football. When I turned back Tuukula was smiling, then sipping his tea, brushing a strange object, like a clear leather sac the size of his palm, hanging from a long length of fishing line from the ceiling.

"How is the tea?" he asked.

"It's good," I said. "Surprisingly, good. I usually drink coffee."

"Latte?"

"Yes." I laughed. "How did you know?"

Tuukula batted the skin sac to one side and it pendulumed slowly between us, defying gravity in long, slow arcs. "The clothes you wear…"

"It's my uniform," I said, slightly mesmerised by the arc of the beige and veined sac.

"The *way* you wear your uniform," he said. "Your hair. The smartphone in your pocket." Tuukula shrugged as I instinctively pressed my palm to my jacket pocket. "These things, make you look like someone who drinks latte." Tuukula smiled as he raised his mug in a gentle toast. "I drink tea."

Luui twitched in my lap as she snored, stretching her legs – longer than they first appeared – over the finger-bitten arm of the chair. I lifted my arm and held my tea above her leg, while stroking her gritty hair with my free hand.

"You said Isaja is her brother?"

"Was," Tuukula said. "I believe Isaja is dead."

8

I have always considered myself Greenlandic. Even in my darkest moments, when the older children teased me at school, calling me the *Danish girl*, I would look at my skin, often darker than theirs with their Danish genes, my long jet black hair and my fierce brown, almost black eyes hard as hazelnuts, cracking with conviction that I *was* Greenlandic. That I *am* Greenlandic. But in that tiny wooden cabin, just a stone's throw from the sea ice, dust clinging to my boots and a small child snoring in my lap, I questioned my identity, wondered what I was missing, why the so-called simple life of the hunter and his family confounded me so.

Tuukula caught the query in my eyes and laughed softly. He finished his tea, stood up, and quietly plucked the enamel mug from my hands, saying, "More tea. There is much to tell."

Luui slept in my lap, and I brushed her hair at each twitch of her limbs, wondering when I might return to Nuuk, when I was expected. One thought did make me smile, as I pictured Sergeant Jowls scowling at the duty roster, perhaps even taking an extra shift to cover for the girl for whom training was very much over.

"You're smiling," Tuukula said, as he pressed the handle of a fresh mug of tea into my hand, the dried orange together with the thin black leaves of herbs and tea pricked the insides of my nose.

"Yes."

"That's good," he said. "It's important to be comfortable before a long tale. Are you comfortable?" Tuukula gestured at his daughter.

"I think my legs are asleep," I said, with a glance at Luui. She had her father's nose, slightly bent, but less gnarly. "I'm fine," I said. "Tell me about Isaja."

"Isaja," Tuukula said, as he sat down, "was a curious boy with a quick mind." Tuukula tapped his head with the middle finger of his right hand, a thimble-length shorter than it was supposed to be. I wondered if he lost the tip in a hunting accident, but he interrupted that thought with a description of Isaja: tall for his age, thin hair, but wiry black like his skin, darker than many of the other children. "His quick mind made him quick with his fists. He had to be. Children can be wicked."

"Yes," I said, thinking back to my own schooling in Nuuk, and the dark winter nights in the children's home, when emotions were charged, running on rocket fuel.

"The teachers called him difficult, but what did they know?" Tuukula shook his head. "Nothing. But Aluusaq, *he* knew. *His* genes. Trace them all the way back to the explorers, that black man who came with Peary? More smarts," Tuukula said, with another stubby tap of his finger to his head. "Aluusaq's son, Isaja's father, was a bad man."

"Was?"

"He's gone," Tuukula said, with a curt nod of

his head. "Rassi left after a fight."

"Sounds like there's a lot of fighting here," I said.

"Only when people are drunk. But Rassi drank a lot, and Isaja spent a lot of time with his *ata*. But he loved his father all the same. For when Rassi was sober he was a great hunter. He had the eye," Tuukula said, pressing his stubby finger to his right eye. "He could spot narwhal from far away, see the tusks fencing in the water, parting the smoke, the condensation, you know? He was always the first into the water. His *qajaq* was always strapped to his sledge, or on his boat, when they sledged the boats to the edge of the ice. Rassi was the fastest in a *qajaq*. He did everything better and faster than everyone else."

"Including drinking?" I asked.

"*Aap.*"

Tuukula fell silent as he curled his hand around the skin sac. He pinched the fishing line between finger and thumb and tugged the line from the tack securing it to the wooden rafters in the ceiling. The sac darkened in Tuukula's hand, as if filling with rich smoke the colour of chocolate, or blood. I stared at the sac, now dark, in his palm, curious at the smile on his face. But the smile turned, the lines of his mouth flattened, and he burst the sac in his hand. I flinched, expecting smoke, but seeing just the shadow of Tuukula's skin blocking the light from the sac.

"Magic," he said, and the light from the fjord blistered through the salt crystals webbing the glass, tickling the sheen of his eye. "I can do tricks, but

Isaja tried to perform the greatest trick of all."

Luui stirred at her brother's name. She tilted her head, casting a sleepy glance at my face, before resting again, heavy lids closing on young eyes.

"What did he do?" I asked. "What trick?"

I forgot all about taking notes. Tuukula's illusion with the skin sac, and his description of Isaja and his father, Rassi the hunter, hooked me with words and images of thick ice, black smoking seas, and tusked whales.

"Isaja knew that when his father caught a narwhal, the whale was butchered, the squares of skin – *Mattak* – shared, then only the tooth remained. As soon as Rassi sold the tooth, the drinking would begin. The day Isaja went missing, Rassi came home with a double tooth, two tusks from the same whale. Rare? Yes," he nodded. "And worth more than double the price of a single tooth. Isaja knew a little magic – he had watched me often enough – and he thought he could do magic that night. He thought he could make the double tooth disappear."

"You mean he stole it?" I said, as the image of a young boy racing through the gravel streets, cradling two white tusks taller than he was, flitted through my mind.

"Isaja did not steal the teeth," Tuukula said. "His magic backfired. Not only did the teeth disappear, but so did Isaja."

"That's when he went missing?"

Tuukula nodded. "Almost twelve months ago to this day."

9

I expected the light to fade, but the warm yellows and burnt orange rays of the spring Arctic sun, bathed the mountains and shone from the glass and aluminium chimney stacks of the houses in Qaanaaq late into the night. I missed the political rally, the Q&A in the sports hall, and the barbecue seal that followed. I also missed my flight, hearing the heavy buzz of the De Havilland Dash 7's four propellers cutting through the thick evening air. Tuukula gently lifted Luui from my lap sometime later in the early evening, laying her in her tiny bed beside his in the room next to the kitchen. He showed me the bathroom bucket, when I asked, and then made more tea, drinking it outside as I freshened up with a bowl of cool water. I joined Tuukula outside on a sun-bitten bench as he smoked a hand-rolled cigarette.

"One a day," he said, flicking ash from the cigarette. "Sometimes two if I'm travelling."

"You were telling me about the day Isaja disappeared," I said, as I sat down beside him. The old wood creaked under our combined weight, bringing a smile to Tuukula's lips.

"It was a night like this," he said, waving his hand towards the ice edge, as if brushing the coast with his fingertips. "There were seven sledges. The hunters had caught three narwhals. They butchered them far out on the ice." Tuukula grinned. "They would have had a hell of a time keeping the dogs in check, all that meat, the stink of blood. They would be going crazy. But they can't run on full bellies. The hunters fed them once they got back. Isaja stood there," Tuukula said, pointing to a gap between two grey frames of wood. "His father's drying racks. He waited there. He had that shuffle that kids do when they are half excited and half scared. Something good is coming, they know that, the whole town talks about it. But there is always a downside." Tuukula pinched the end of his cigarette, flaking the last paper and tobacco into the grit and dust at his feet. "Isaja saw his father. He waved. And then he saw the tusks."

"You saw Isaja that night?" I asked.

"*Aap.*" Tuukula pointed. "Standing right there."

"And you saw where he went? After that?" I pulled my notebook from my pocket, turning to a fresh page as Tuukula spoke.

"Isaja helped his father with the dogs. He put each of them on the chain. Isaja's mother," Tuukula said, with a brief smile. "Is Luui's mother too. She helped carry the meat. More people helped. There were a lot of people." Tuukula traced his hand over imaginary heads in front of where we sat. "That was when Isaja disappeared. I didn't think anything of it. But he was gone, and so were the teeth." Tuukula turned slightly to face me, his bony knees bumping mine. "This is the interesting part, the real magic. Isaja took the teeth."

"Yes," I said. "Both of them."

"That's right. But maybe you haven't seen narwhal teeth?"

"I have," I said, thinking about the creamy ivory tusks I had seen in the souvenir shops in Nuuk, and the giant tusks, dry, flaked and cracked behind glass in the museum. "They are all sizes."

"And some are taller than we are." Tuukula nodded. "But a hunter will bring back the head of a narwhal, cut flat, standing up with the teeth pointing into the sky, still attached." Tuukula bent his left arm at right angles, tapping his elbow with the stub of his right index finger. "Imagine the head, here, about the size of two small tyres and just as heavy. Then the teeth," he said, tracing his finger up his arm. "Taller than Isaja." Tuukula relaxed and reached for his tea. "Real magic," he said. "Better than mine, for how else can a seven-year-old boy carry a narwhal head with a double tusk off the beach and out of the village?"

"He had help?" I said.

"Maybe he did." Tuukula shrugged. "But no one saw him or the teeth again." Tuukula tipped his head back and swallowed the last dregs of his tea. "I'm getting old," he said, the late sun twinkled in his eye and cast a warm glow on his wrinkled face. "I drink to keep me lubricated, and the more I drink, the more I have to pee, which keeps me moving." Tuukula grinned as he stood up. "You can sleep in my bed. I'll sleep on the couch."

"I can stay at the hotel," I said.

"Closed," he said. "For the spring. You can have my bed." Tuukula burped and patted his chest. "Luui creeps under the covers in the early morning.

Just so you know. Kiss her head and hold her hand and she falls right asleep." The light caught his eye again as he chuckled. "She farts," he said.

"Okay," I said, frowning at the curious detail. "That's good to know."

I checked my smartphone for messages as Tuukula stretched his legs, weaving between the drying racks on his way to the sea ice. It occurred to me that my usual city girl sensibilities had been disarmed, as if they had been turned off by the gentle and intimate family nature of Tuukula and his young daughter. I felt adopted, almost, and I discovered a gentle warmth flooding through my body as I sat in the glow of the High Arctic sun, texting Atii that I was roughing it, and that she would have to do without me for a few more days. In truth, I had no idea how many.

10

Luui pressed her knee into my nose as she crawled out of bed, dragging the duvet with her as if it was an oversized comfort blanket. I sighed, rubbed the sleep from my eyes and dressed, blinking into the morning sun, curious that it should be so strong already. Clearly, I wasn't quite prepared for spring in the far north of Greenland. I dressed quickly and quietly, draping my heavy police jacket over the back of the armchair as I padded through the living room, following the sounds of Luui's excited chatter into the kitchen. I caught the word *five* in my limited Greenlandic and remembered that it was her birthday.

"I need to talk to Aluusaq today," I said, as Tuukula pressed a cup of coffee into my hand.

"It's black, unless you want long-life milk," he said, with a nod to a tiny fridge shuddering in the corner.

"Black is fine," I said. Luui curled one hand into mine, tugging me to one of two seats pressed up against the wall. The kitchen table lay flat, hinged against the wall with robust screws of assorted sizes and heads. Luui pushed my knees to one side with grubby palms, turning me away from the table until she could lift it and prop it up with a square leg of wood. I put my coffee down on the surface as Luui beamed at me. "Aluusaq," I said, as Tuukula cracked eggs into a frying pan. "Where can I find him?"

"Luui will take you," he said. "I need time to tidy up and bake the cakes for her *kaffemik*."

"*Kaffemik!*" Luui said, twirling in the tiny space between me and the electric hob where Tuukula fried the eggs. She twirled into my legs, bumping the table with her head, before crawling into my lap with her hand pressed to her temple.

"Let me see," I said, peeling away her fingers to blow on her forehead. Luui laughed and I blew some more, pushing her hair one way and then the other until Tuukula clicked his fingers and pointed at the bathroom door. Luui slipped off my lap and disappeared into the bathroom.

"She has to wash," Tuukula said. "Then I'll fix her hair, find a dress and send her with you to Aluusaq."

"Her grandfather?"

"*Naamik*." Tuukula shook his head. "Aluusaq was Rassi's father, Isaja's *ata*."

I checked my notes as Tuukula slid a plate onto the table – fried egg with mushrooms from a glass jar, heaped on top of a piece of square toast, buttered thickly. He served three helpings, then called for Luui to hurry before sitting down opposite me. Luui crawled onto Tuukula's lap, reaching between his arms for a fork. I smiled at the sight of father and daughter eating, with four arms, two mouths and a lot of wriggling; Luui bounced as she ate.

Tuukula picked at a knot in Luui's hair, then

sent her back into the bathroom to clean her teeth. I stood up, fixed my ponytail, and then left Tuukula at the table. I knocked on the bathroom door and as I opened it I saw Luui standing on an upturned crate while brushing her teeth. I leaned around her, pulling my own toothbrush and paste from my pocket. She held up her brush and I squeezed a fat worm of paste onto it. Luui's eyes widened as she tasted it. When Luui finished brushing her teeth, she stared at me in the mirror taped to the wall, and I stood behind her, teasing her hair into long, smooth lengths with a brush I found beside the mug of toothbrushes and wrinkled tubes of toothpaste.

"How about a ponytail?" I said, tilting my head to one side and letting my hair fall over my shoulder. Luui nodded, plucking at the light blue sleeves of my police shirt as I found a spare elastic in my pocket, slipping my fingers through it, before rolling it to the base of Luui's ponytail. I smiled as she chattered away, catching less than half of what she said as the Qaanaaq dialect proved even more difficult than the West Greenlandic I heard most days. The consonants were softer, more edible and swallowed faster than I could fathom.

"Luui," Tuukula called from the kitchen. "Clothes," he added, in Danish.

"*Aap*," she said, slipping off the crate and whirling into the kitchen.

I stayed by the mirror, curious at the smile curling one side of my mouth, as I remembered another little girl, not unlike Luui; only I couldn't remember having so much energy when *I* was five.

"Hello," I whispered to my reflection, as I fast-forwarded to the present. "This is the Missing Persons desk. How can I help you?" The truth was I had no idea, but my new job was certainly varied, if a little short on creature comforts. "*You're roughing it, girl*," I said, in my best imitation of Atii's big-city-girl slang.

"Luui's waiting outside," Tuukula said, as I thanked him for breakfast. "Bring her back at two o'clock."

"Tuukula," I said. "I'm investigating Isaja's disappearance, not babysitting Luui."

"*Aap*," he said, eyes twinkling in the early morning light. "Try not to be late."

11

A day later than planned and one day over schedule, Luui led me up a flight of two low steps and onto the bruised wooden deck of a white-walled house. Flaps of bitumen at the corners of the roof waved in the wind coming off the ice cap, sending a chill past my collar and down my neck, cooling my irritation at Tuukula – using me to look after his daughter – as my curiosity was piqued. Luui rapped her tiny knuckles on the door, reached up for the handle and stepped inside Aluusaq's house. I followed, pressing toe to heel as I removed my boots, in a similar action to Luui. I heard her greet Aluusaq as I tugged my notebook from my jacket pocket, before stepping into the living room. The thin old man hunched and folded into a lawn chair was not who I had expected.

Aluusaq's eyes were charcoal grey when they should have been dark brown. His skin, parched and crevassed like a dried fish, was brittle to the touch when I shook his hand. He nodded to the chair beside him and I sat down as Luui settled on the couch. Aluusaq spoke softly, as if his words were blowing from off the ice cap, like the wind, but warmer as he expressed his surprise that I was sitting in his living room, actively investigating the case of his missing grandson.

"The local police would look into it if you asked them," I said.

"They have, and they found nothing," Aluusaq said, the words rattling out of his thin frame. "When I called Nuuk, I asked specifically for the Missing Persons desk. I knew they would have to respond, and now you're here."

He said something to Luui, waving vaguely in the direction of the kitchen, while I wondered how much I should tell him, about how little he could expect, especially twelve months after Isaja went missing.

"Why did you wait so long to report him missing?" I asked.

"I didn't. I reported it straight away. But Rassi said Isaja was hiding, and that he would be back soon. I wanted to believe my son."

"And now?"

Aluusaq wiped at his cheek, although his eyes seemed too dry for tears. He smiled at Luui as she returned from the kitchen, the tip of her tongue clamped between her lips, as she carried two glasses of water, clogged with ice beneath the lip of each glass. Her shoulders sagged as I took one of the glasses, and she reached up to Aluusaq with the second. Luui scurried back into the kitchen before I could thank her. I sipped the water, frowning slightly at the hint of cold salt on my lips.

"From the sea," Aluusaq said. "The children bring me ice from the icebergs to cool my drinks. Luui knows where I keep it." Aluusaq smiled again. "You only taste the salt once."

"Yes," I said, putting my glass down. "You said

Rassi said Isaja was just hiding?"

"*Aap*."

"For how long did you believe him?"

Aluusaq wiped a second time at his cheek. Several breaths rattled in and out of his lungs before he spoke. "A long time," he said, quietly. "Too long."

"Did Rassi visit you during that time?"

"Once a week. Sometimes more if he needed money."

"And you asked him about Isaja?"

"Every time."

"And what did he say?"

"That he was staying with friends or living with his mother."

"And was he?"

"Isaja's mother lives in Ilulissat. I don't know her number."

Aluusaq looked out of the south-facing window, and I imagined him staring as far as Ilulissat, searching for his grandson. If I had known that Isaja's mother was in Ilulissat, I might have stopped on the way.

"He's not there," Aluusaq said. "Not in Ilulissat."

"How can you be sure?"

"I can't, but no one remembers Isaja leaving. That's the only thing everybody agrees on, when they talk about him. They are talking about him again, now that you have come." Aluusaq caught my eye, staring at me, searching for something with the same intense gaze he had when staring south in search of his grandson. "They think you have come to arrest me."

"Why would they think that?"

"Because," Aluusaq said, brushing his dry cheeks with a crooked finger, "they know what everybody knows, that Isaja is dead."

"And why do they think I've come to arrest you?"

"Because before my son died, he told everyone in Qaanaaq that I killed Isaja."

12

"My son was a great hunter," Aluusaq said. He pointed his crooked finger at a picture hanging on the wall, and I walked around the couch to look at it. Aluusaq's words followed me, describing the ghosts in the photograph. "He had the strongest dogs, the fastest *qajaq*, and the keenest eye. He could see..."

"Narwhals fencing at the very edge of the ice," I whispered, my face pressed close to the photograph, as Aluusaq sang the familiar praises of his son. I was curious as to what I should think about Rassi, the great hunter, the great drinker. Twice now, I had heard men complement Rassi on his prowess as a hunter, and both men – Tuukula first, and now Aluusaq – had also described the other Rassi, the one who scared his son so much he fled the village with the double narwhal tooth.

I looked at the man in the photograph, imagining a younger Aluusaq in his stead, with a thick head of black hair, bushy black eyebrows protruding above keen eyes in a sun-beaten face. The boy standing beside Rassi in the photo was no taller than Luui – perhaps the same age when the photo was taken. While Rassi looked straight at the camera, Isaja looked up at his father. There was a depth in the boy's eyes suggesting he had seen too much, and that he could see into the future.

"Isaja was four and half when they took that picture," Aluusaq said.

I made a note in my notebook and returned to sit beside Aluusaq, glimpsing Luui, just visible in the kitchen, playing with a jigsaw puzzle at the kitchen table as I sat down.

"Aluusaq," I said. "What happened to your son?"

The old man gave a slow shrug. "No one knows. He disappeared, like Isaja. People say he went through the ice."

"Where?"

"On the way to Siorapaluk. Fifty kilometres," Aluusaq said, pointing. "To the north and west."

"He was never found?"

"No."

"Then why do people say he went through the ice?"

"Because they found his team. The dogs ran all the way to Siorapaluk."

"Did they search for him?"

"It was mid-winter." Aluusaq shook his head. "Minus fifty. It was crazy to make the journey. The wind was blowing."

"But if it was minus fifty," I said. "Wouldn't the ice be thick?"

"There is one place," Aluusaq said. "Where the ice is always thin. The tide runs quickly there, eating away at the ice in the bay. You can be unlucky," Aluusaq said. "I think Rassi was unlucky."

The old man looked away and I expected him to

wipe at a dry tear on his parched cheeks. But he kept his fingers in his lap, clenched, as if suppressing something.

"But what about his dogs?" I said. "You said they ran all the way to Siorapaluk. They must have crossed the ice."

"He would have cut the sledge from the traces," Aluusaq said. "They came in a fan of dogs. But no sledge."

"This was mid-winter?"

"*Aap*."

"Earlier this year?"

Aluusaq nodded. "In February."

I sucked at my teeth as I did a quick calculation. It was May. Isaja had been missing for nearly a year. He went missing *last* May, before the ice broke up. But his father, Rassi, didn't die until February the following year, if he died at all.

"Rassi told you Isaja was hiding, or with his mother in Ilulissat," I said, pressing the tip of my pen to a clean page in my notebook. "And you believed him, for ten months, before Rassi went missing. Is that right?"

Aluusaq held my gaze and nodded, just once.

"But before he left, Rassi told people here that you killed his son."

Another nod.

I looked at Aluusaq, curious for a moment as to *how* he might have killed anybody when he couldn't even fetch ice from the sea for his water.

"Ten months after your grandson goes missing," I said, tapping my pen on the page. "Your son goes missing, presumed dead."

"*Aap*," Aluusaq said.

"But you waited three more months before calling the police in Nuuk."

I gripped the pen and the notebook in my hand, reaching for my glass to take a sip of salty water. Aluusaq watched me, waited for me to swallow before he spoke.

"And you want to know why?" he said, as I put down my glass.

"Yes," I said.

Aluusaq glanced at the photograph on the wall before continuing. "I had given up all hope," he said, after a long, rattling breath. "But then something happened that gave me the strength to look again, just one more time, before my time is done."

"And what was that, Aluusaq? What happened?"

Aluusaq paused, and then said, "Somebody tried to sell a narwhal tooth to one of the Danish teachers in Qaanaaq. It was a double tooth."

"Isaja's tooth," I said, with a click of my pen.

"*Aap*," Aluusaq said, and for a moment, his eyes darkened, flooding the sickly grey with a vibrant flush of brown, the same eyes as his son and grandson, the eyes of a hunter.

13

I pressed Aluusaq for more details, but he knew little more, only that a Greenlander tried to sell the tooth to a temporary teacher.

"But you don't know who he is?"

"*Naamik.*"

"What about the name of the teacher?" I asked, but Aluusaq shook his head.

Luui appeared in the doorway. She padded across the floor, slipped her tiny hand into mine, and gave me a gentle but insistent tug. I checked the time on my smartphone and nodded. It was almost two o'clock. Aluusaq nodded when I told him I would be in touch, and again when I said he should contact me if he remembered anything, if he heard anything, or if something new occurred that he thought might be relevant. Confident that I had covered all the bases, I tugged my boots on and stepped out of Aluusaq's house, blinking into the sun and squinting after Luui as she bounded down the steps. She stopped beside the familiar dark blue police Toyota, hands on her hips as she stared up at Constable Umeerinneq.

"Did he tell you anything?" Umeerinneq asked, as I stepped off Aluusaq's deck and joined them in the street.

"Background information," I said.

"About his son disappearing in February?"

"Yes."

"And his grandson in May last year."

"He told me that, and how Rassi said he killed Isaja."

Umeerinneq shook his head. "Aluusaq has been sick for nearly two years now. He's too weak to do much more than sit in that chair. The council has a helper get him up in the morning, make his meals, and put him to bed at night." Umeerinneq shrugged. "Aluusaq didn't kill anybody."

"No," I said. "But he feels responsible." I pulled out my notebook and laid it flat on the bonnet of the patrol car, beckoning for Umeerinneq to come closer as I flipped through the pages. Luui tugged at the cargo pocket of my trousers, and I reached down to hold her hand, saying, "Just a minute," as I pointed at my notes about the man trying to sell the tooth.

"A double tooth?"

"That's what Aluusaq said."

"I never heard about that, but a lot can happen in the winter that just seeps out into the dark. Easy to miss when you're alone," Umeerinneq said.

"But you must know someone who might have tried to sell a tooth?"

"There's this one guy," Umeerinneq said. He took a pen from the sleeve pocket on his jacket, writing a name in block capitals in my notepad. "Peter Ulloriaq," he said. "I can try and rustle him up. Although, I haven't seen him for a few days."

"Hunting?"

"Peter?" Umeerinneq laughed. "No, too lazy.

Plus, he's got a few problems – only one eye and a limp. Left leg, I think." Umeerinneq looked down as Luui tugged once more at my trousers. "You found a friend."

"Yes," I said, slipping my notebook into my jacket pocket. "And it's her birthday. We're late for her *kaffemik*. She's Tuukula's daughter."

"Tuukula?"

"Yes. I stayed there last night."

Umeerinneq caught my eye and then looked away. "Yeah, I'm sorry about that. I should have offered you a place to stay, but I got caught up with the politicians. They kept me busy, and it was late before I remembered you were here."

"It's fine. No problem," I said. "But I think we have to go."

"I'll give you a ride," he said, opening the Toyota's rear passenger door. Umeerinneq said something to Luui and she clambered into the patrol car. He helped her with her seatbelt, shut the door and then gestured for me to get in. "Tuukula is an interesting man," Umeerinneq said, as he started the engine.

"He's a hunter," I said.

"Well, yes, he hunts," Umeerinneq said. "But he's not really a hunter. He's something else."

"What?" I said, as Umeerinneq frowned. "You can't tell me?"

Umeerinneq looked in the rear-view mirror, angling it down to see Luui as he said something in Greenlandic.

"*Angakkoq*," she said. Luui stretched her arm outwards and opened her tiny fist with a flash of fingers. "*Poof*," she said, and then, in English, "Magic."

"Your *ataata* is a magician?" I asked, furrowing my brow with another trademark frown.

"Not a magician," Umeerinneq said. "Tuukula is a shaman."

14

Luui leaped out of the patrol car as soon as Umeerinneq opened the door. She bustled into the crowd of children playing outside the door of her home, grinning as they pressed small coins into her palms, sometimes a bar of chocolate, sometimes something bigger. I realised I had nothing and wondered what I should give.

"People up here give what they can," Umeerinneq said, as if reading my thoughts. "It doesn't have to be much. A few coins, five kroner, maybe twenty. If you give too much," he said, as I pulled a fifty kroner note from my pocket, "it could send the wrong signal."

"I'll give it her later," I said.

"Sure."

Umeerinneq followed me past the children and inside Tuukula's cabin. The chairs were pushed right up to the walls, and a small table – just two crates with a broad plank of grey, flaky wood between them – supported three huge chocolate cakes with sugar frosting, all the more impressive when compared with the meagre surroundings. The cabin smelt of chocolate, coffee and fish, the oiliest fish I could ever remember smelling, or tasting, when Tuukula pressed a Swiss Army knife into my hand and pointed at the fish on the flat cardboard box on the kitchen floor. I cut a thick cube of raw white meat from the flat fish, licking at the oil on my lips, grinning at Tuukula who took the knife from my hand and passed it to one of the other guests. There were four adults and two small children crouched around the fish, and a fifth person, a middle-aged man, sitting on one of the two chairs in the kitchen.

"Peter Ulloriaq," Umeerinneq said, as the man stared at us.

Peter took one look at Umeerinneq, before bolting for the back door.

He moved faster than I expected for a man with a limp. Nor did his limited eyesight slow him down. Peter weaved around the empty oil cans rusting behind Tuukula's cabin, ducked through a gap in the tall picket fence, separating the row of hunting and fishing cabins along the beach front from the water tower and oil tank behind them. Umeerinneq called out for Peter to stop, as I slipped through the picket fence and gave chase.

"I'll get the car," Umeerinneq shouted.

I shouted something back, then pressed my hand around the grip of my pistol, something I instinctively did when running. I chided myself about it, thinking that I should learn how best to wear my belt and holster, then forgot all about it again, as Peter speeded up.

Peter's mistake was trying to climb the gantry running around the water tower, jumping up to reach for the lowest rung of the ladder to pull it down to the ground. I tumbled into him, throwing him off balance and sending a cloud of dust and grit into our hair and faces. Peter spat grit from his mouth as he rolled away from me.

"Stop," I said, brushing strands of gritty hair from my face. "Peter, we just want to talk to you."

Peter scrabbled to his feet, waving me off and staggering down a stony bank back towards the picket fence. I heard the patrol car, stones plinging against the panels, as Umeerinneq sped along the road, blocking Peter's path.

I slowed as Peter leaned, bent double, against the picket fence, chest heaving, hands pressed to his knees. He lifted his chin, glared at me with his one good eye, then spat a stream of dusty phlegm into the dirt.

"I've done nothing wrong," he said, in Danish.

"I know." I stopped just a few metres away, catching my breath, and letting my hands dangle at my sides, keeping them clear of my pistol and cuffs. "But you might know something that can help me find a boy."

"I don't know anything about Isaja."

"Isaja?" I said, as Umeerinneq approached from the other side of Peter. "What do you know about him?"

"Rassi's son?" Peter said. "You're looking for him?" He glanced at Umeerinneq and then spat one more time. "Everyone's talking about it. Ever since Aluusaq made the call to Nuuk. Now you're here."

"That's right," Umeerinneq said. "Now she's here, maybe you can tell her what you never told me, eh?"

"I don't know where the boy is."

"Okay," I said. "But what about the tooth?" I

took a step closer. "Do you know anything about a narwhal tooth?"

"A double tooth," Umeerinneq added.

Peter straightened his back. He nodded as he leaned against the fence. "*Aap*," he said. "I found a tooth, a double tooth, like you say, and I tried to sell it."

"Where did you find it?" I asked.

Peter lifted his hand and straightened a bony finger. He pointed north, and said, "On the way to Siorapaluk."

15

Umeerinneq said he would drive Peter home once he had answered my questions. He described an old derelict hut, located above a small bay on the way to Siorapaluk.

"No one goes there," he said, dusting himself off as I started a fresh page in my notepad.

"Then why did you?"

"I was with Sakiusi, a hunter. We were coming back from Siorapaluk. He said it was a place where polar bears had denned, and he wanted to see if there were any tracks in the area. I was cold. I told him to leave me at the hut."

"And you went inside?"

Peter shook his head. "It's a bad place. I didn't want to go inside."

"So, you didn't see anyone?"

"I waited by the snowmobile for Sakiusi to finish looking."

"But you found a narwhal tooth?"

"*Aap*," Peter said, with a nod. "Wrapped in a plastic tarp, half buried under a pile of rocks, like it was on top of a grave. The wind had blown the snow off it. The tarp was flapping. I took a look, found the tooth – both of them. And then Sakiusi came back."

"And you brought the tooth back to Qaanaaq?"

"*Aap*." Peter looked at Umeerinneq. "I didn't steal it. I found it."

Peter said nothing more. Umeerinneq nodded at the car, sliding one of the broken slats in the fence to one side as Peter stepped through it.

"I'll catch you later," he said.

I waved, waited until they had driven away, and then walked back to Tuukula's house. There were new faces at the *kaffemik*, filling the cabin with shuffles and a quiet chatter between sawing meat from the fish, and calling for more coffee. Tuukula met me at the back door, grinning as he pointed at two plastic garden chairs just to one side.

"I need a break," he said, as he rolled a cigarette on his knee. "They can get their own coffee."

"How's Luui?"

"How is she, or where is she?"

"Where, I suppose." I slipped my hand in my pocket. "I have something for her."

"Give it to her later," Tuukula said. He lit his cigarette and then lifted his chin, nodding at the picket fence behind us. "What happened with Peter?"

"I thought he could help with the investigation. Aluusaq said a man tried to sell a narwhal tooth, like the one you said Isaja stole from his father."

"He made it disappear," Tuukula said. "There's a difference."

"Okay," I said. "But it's possible that Peter made that same tooth disappear from a cabin further north."

"On the way to Siorapaluk?"

"Yes. You know it?"

"I know where it is."

"Of course, you do," I said.

Tuukula smoked as I wrestled with an idea in my head. I needed to see the cabin, that much was clear, but I was already overdue. A message beeped into my smartphone, and I glanced at it, swiping it to one side as soon as I saw the sender's name.

"A friend?" Tuukula asked.

"My superior, Sergeant Jowls."

"Howls?"

"*Jowls*," I said, laughing as I pretended to pinch rolls of fat around my neck. "His real name is Duneq."

"And what does he want?"

"He says I have to come back to Nuuk."

"Wednesday," Tuukula said. "That's the next flight, weather depending."

I checked the date on my phone, biting my lip as I made my decision.

"I want to see the cabin."

Tuukula raised his eyebrows, just once, then started to roll a second cigarette. "For later," he said, tucking it behind his ear when he was finished.

"Tuukula, did you hear what I said?"

"That you want to go to the hut?" He nodded. "I heard you."

"And?"

He waved as Luui opened the back door. "I think you will find answers there," he said, as Luui bounced across the dirt and into his lap.

"But I don't know how to get there, and even if I did, I don't think my budget will stretch to a helicopter." I laughed at the word *budget* wondering if I even had one.

"But you want to go?"

"I think I owe it to Isaja and his grandfather."

"He won't like what you might find there."

"But you think I'll find something? Don't you?"

"*Aap*," Tuukula said.

"And you know the way?"

"I do."

"Tuukula…"

Luui fidgeted on Tuukula's lap. He brushed her fringe to one side, curled his finger inside her ponytail, and then kissed her on the forehead. Luui leaned against Tuukula's chest, reaching for the cigarette behind his ear, giggling when he swatted at her fingers.

"We will take you," Tuukula said, tickling Luui. She giggled off his lap and he tapped her lightly on the bottom, sending her back into the cabin as a new wave of guests replaced the last.

"*We*?" I said.

"*Aap*, Luui and me. It is a long way, but we have the sun, we can sledge through the night."

"Sledge? You don't have a snowmobile?"

"I do have a snowmobile," Tuukula said.

He pointed at something hidden just behind the oil barrels, and I sighed at the sight of a broken windshield, a bent ski, and a seat that looked like it had been nibbled by a giant mouse.

"Puppies," Tuukula said, when he saw where I was looking. "But now they are grown, and they've grown strong." He stood up, plucked the cigarette from behind his ear, and stuck it between his lips. "I sometimes have two," he said. "When I'm travelling." He lit the cigarette, puffed a small cloud of smoke above his head, and then pointed to the north. "Constable Jensen," he said. "Let's find you some proper clothes. We leave tonight."

16

Luui took my hand and guided me around Tuukula's long, broad sledge, pointing out the different parts, as I fiddled with the straps holding up the polar bear skin trousers Tuukula insisted that I wear. However dishevelled his cabin might appear, the shaman's sledging clothes, gear and dogs seemed to be of the highest quality – to my ignorant eyes, at least. Luui rattled off another string of long Greenlandic words, quite unperturbed at my limited grasp of her language. She started on the dogs next, calling out each name in English. I caught the name of the last two of fifteen dogs as I followed her to the head of the team.

"Cargo?" I asked, pointing at the large white male just behind the lead dog.

"Cargo very bad," Luui said, in English. The ears of her hood wiggled as she shook her head. Her hood had fascinated me earlier, sewn from dog fur with real dog ears, soft and pointed.

"And that one?" I pointed at the lead dog.

"Spirit," Luui said. She took my hand again, skirting around Cargo and pulling me all the way to the head of the team where she promptly let go and pulled Spirit into a generous hug. Cargo growled behind us until the arrival of Umeerinneq's patrol car bumping over the ice foot and onto the sea ice distracted the big sledge dog.

A chill wind followed in the wake of the patrol car and I tugged at the collar of my sealskin smock, pulling the hood over my head as Umeerinneq stepped out of the car.

"I can guess where you're headed and I don't suppose I can stop you," he said, as he walked across the ice.

"The answers are at the cabin," I said. "Everything points in that direction."

"There's trouble in that direction, too." Umeerinneq paused at a shout from Tuukula, calling for Luui to help him. "It's May. The ice might be thick here, but further up the coast, where the tide is stronger, it will be weaker, more dangerous."

"I'll be fine," I said, brushing my hair to one side as the wind caught it.

"Okay," Umeerinneq said. "But just one more thing – your boss called."

"The commissioner."

"No." He frowned. "The other one. Sergeant Duneq. He wanted me to remind you that you don't have a budget for this, and that you are overstepping your authority."

"Did he say training was over, too?"

"What?"

"Nothing," I said. Nuuk felt very far away, and the sergeant's words seemed less weighty than usual. I felt a surge of giddiness at the thought that I was beyond the sergeant's reach, tempered only by the butterflies in my stomach at the thought of sledging north across thin ice, towards Siorapaluk.

"Constable?" Tuukula said.

I started at the sound of his voice, wondering how he could move so quietly. He pointed at Luui sitting on a canvas kitbag lashed across the thwarts at the front of the sledge, and I nodded.

"I'm ready," I said.

"What about your pistol?" Umeerinneq asked. "For bears."

"A pistol is no good," Tuukula said. He pointed at a long, soft leather case tied to one of the uprights at the back of the sledge. "I have a rifle."

"And my pistol is somewhere inside all these layers," I said, curious that I couldn't feel it, let alone find it. I hoped I wouldn't need it.

Tuukula clapped Umeerinneq on the shoulder, and said, "We'll be back before Wednesday. Don't worry. I'll look after your constable."

I almost laughed, settled for a smile, and then followed Tuukula back to the sledge, skirting wide around Cargo as the big dog glared at me. Tuukula pointed at a spot on the sledge behind Luui, then tugged a band of bone with two slits carved through the centre of it. He pushed the bone into Luui's hands, then helped her tie the sealskin cord around the back of her head.

"Sunglasses," he said. "From the old days."

The sun circled low in the sky, and the reflection on the ice was far softer than the middle of the day. I had the impression the Greenlandic sunglasses at this hour served another purpose, much like the aviator glasses Tuukula wore in the car. Tuukula confirmed it as he pulled out another pair, grinning as he fixed them in place, before quietly releasing the quick release anchor frozen into the ice.

The dogs twitched as Tuukula climbed onto the sledge. He hushed them with a growl, fidgeting behind me as he tugged the dog whip out from beneath a cord of sealskin.

"Ready," he whispered to Luui.

"Ready steady," she whispered back. Luui raised her hand, pressing a small thumb into the air.

"Hold onto my daughter," Tuukula said, as Luui let her hand drop.

"*Go*," she shouted, and the sledge leaped across the ice as the dogs leaned into the traces, clawing behind Spirit as she steered the team north to Siorapaluk.

17

I held on to Luui, but the bumping and grating of the sledge, together with her wriggling back and forth over the kitbag, made me feel like I was trying to catch a basketball rolling across the deck of a boat in wild seas. Tuukula laughed, and I gave up, slipping my hands inside the pouch pocket at the front of my smock, letting the wind tug at my hair. Tuukula reached forwards, pulling the tip of my hood back to reveal my face. The hood fell flat against my neck and the wind flowed through my hair. I pulled the elastic from my ponytail, closed my eyes and revelled in the fresh Arctic breeze, the soft rays of the sun, and the gentle shush and grate of the sledge as the ice smoothed and the dogs found their rhythm. I felt invigorated and empowered by the land, willing to give up some city comforts – just for a little while – as we sank into the wild.

When I opened my eyes again, I found Luui crouched in front of me, staring into my face. She wriggled forwards, cupped her palms on my cheeks and traced my nose, my ears, and my eyes with the tips of her warm fingers. I wrinkled my nose as it tickled, and, when Luui giggled, I wrapped my arm around her, pulled her into my lap, and held on, just as Tuukula had asked me to.

CONSTABLE PETRA JENSEN 1-3

We sledged through the night, as the sun swung behind the mountains, and the light faded just a little. Luui snored in my lap and I dozed in between, lifting my head each time Tuukula asked if I was warm, if I was hungry, if I was content?

Content.

I suppose I was. Out there on the ice, sledging north. But the very idea was so far removed from what I thought I would be doing in my first year as a police constable, it made me wonder. The commissioner would be accused of favouritism and Sergeant Jowls would do his best to derail and sabotage my new-found responsibilities. But in that moment, on Tuukula's sledge, with Luui snoring in my arms, even when she farted into her travelling furs, I realised I could cope with a little favouritism, if that's what it was.

I slept, hunched over Luui, until the dawn light and a slow sledge woke me. Luui was perched at the front of the sledge, watching her father, as Tuukula tickled the dog whip on the ice in front of the team, guiding the way around what looked to be bad ice. Water oozed through holes and cracks, spilling onto the surface, cooling from sea black to frost white as it spread.

"Hey," Tuukula said, as one of the wheel dogs closest to the runners drifted out to the right. "Hey. Hey." He growled when the dog didn't listen, then flicked the whip over the team, striking the ice to one side of the dog. The dog bumped into its neighbour, then yelped as Cargo nipped its flank, bringing the younger dog back into line, before jogging back to the number two position. Tuukula led the team in this way across two bays, before finally stopping the team on a patch of thick ice just off the shore.

"We're close," he said, as he pulled a small primus, pans and matches out of the sledge bag stretched between the two uprights.

I stared into the north, searching for the hut as Tuukula melted snow to make tea. He pressed an enamel mug into my hands, and a strip of dried whale meat into my mouth. Luui chewed at a long strip of meat, tilting her head and tugging at it like a Danish child might chew a strip of candy.

"Do you see it?" Tuukula asked as he sipped his tea.

"Not yet," I said.

I worked my teeth around the whale meat until I could chew. The tea helped.

"There." Tuukula pointed at a flat strip of black just above a white knoll of snow covering a boulder on the land. "That's the roof," he said.

"I see it."

There wasn't much to see, and I was impressed that he knew where to look. But another question nagged at me, and I chewed faster in order to ask it.

"You said Isaja disappeared that night."

"*Aap.*"

"But what you really mean, is that he sledged here, to this cabin."

"*Imaqa*," Tuukula said. "He could have."

"That's quite a feat for a seven-year-old boy," I said.

"Powerful magic." Tuukula dipped his head to smile at Luui. "It runs in the family. It's in their blood."

I didn't doubt it. Nor did I doubt my gut instinct that the answers to Isaja's disappearance could be found in or around the old hut, just a few minutes away by dog sledge. I finished my tea, took another strip of whale meat, and chewed the rest of the way to the hut.

18

Tuukula cut two loops in the ice to anchor the team, settling them with cubes of seal blubber. He stood over them, growling each time one dog tried to steal another dog's fat. I watched, fascinated, as the fat gooped from the dog's incisors and jaws as they chewed, gulped and swallowed. Tuukula waited until each dog was finished, and then walked back to the sledge to pick up the rifle. He slung it over his shoulder and nodded for Luui to walk on ahead.

"The hut is old," he said, as we clambered over the ice foot dividing the land from the frozen sea. "But useful in emergencies."

"But you wouldn't stay there for long?"

"Not unless I had to," Tuukula said. He paused as Luui said something, then beckoned for her to come quickly, stooping to pick her up as he slipped the rifle off his shoulder. Tuukula held Luui in one arm and clasped the rifle in the other, the stock against his hip.

"What is it?" I said, pulling back my hood and tilting my head, almost certain I had heard something on the wind. "Is it a bear?"

The sound of huffing, scraping, and snorting lilted over the snow-covered boulder, pricking Tuukula's senses, and causing Luui to curl her arms around his neck. I tugged at the V of my smock, lifting it before thrusting my hand inside the polar bear skin trousers, worming my fingers to my hip where I found the snap of the holster. I curled my fingers around the pistol grip and pulled it out of my trousers.

The standard issue 9mm Heckler and Koch USP Compact pistol held thirteen rounds. Too small to kill a bear, but I figured I had thirteen chances to scare it away. Long enough to give Tuukula a chance to kill it if need be. I felt my heart leap with skittish beats. I took several breaths, reining in my adrenaline a little, just enough for me to nod at Tuukula and point to the right of the boulder.

"I'll go that way," I said.

"I'll come with you."

I led the way, scuffing the soles of my sealskin *kamikker* over icy boulders, before breaking the crust of wind-leached snow. Tuukula nodded for me to keep going each time I turned to see where he was. The huffing and snorting grew louder, together with another sound, like rocks rolling and crashing to one side.

I reached the boulder and crouched in the snow beside it. The pistol cooled in my grasp and I wondered if I should wear gloves. But the thought vanished at the sound of a hoarse shout and the crack of a bullet zipping through the air towards us. Tuukula dropped onto his belly, flattening Luui in the snow beneath him as he lifted his head. He pointed to one side and I moved to my right as Tuukula slid the rifle into his shoulder, sighting up the rise, ready to fire if the bear were to suddenly lurch around the boulder. I paused at another shout, flinching at a second crack of a rifle.

"I'm going to take a look," I said, ignoring Tuukula as he started to protest.

With my pistol in one hand, I squirmed onto my belly and crawled the last few metres of the rise until I could see over the top. My breath caught in my throat as I saw a gaunt man with a long wispy beard and wavy black hair, naked but for a pair of threadbare *kamikker* on his feet, fiddling with the bolt of the rifle in his hands. I scanned left, away from the man standing in front of the dilapidated hut, then swore at the sight of a polar bear, poised above an exposed shallow grave of rocks, huffing from side to side as the man fired for a third time.

The third shot clapped into the snow in front of the grave, far short of the bear. The bear's creamy, matted flanks showed no signs of it being hit by the first two shots. It roared, rocking back onto its hind legs as I gripped my pistol in two hands, aimed above the bear's head, and fired three shots in quick succession. The bear lurched to one side and I fired another three shots, followed by two more, encouraging the bear as it dropped onto all fours and loped away to one side, before curling back across the land and racing towards the frozen sea.

"Firing," Tuukula said, as walked up beside me, chambered a round in his rifle and shot after the bear. I saw the puff of snow at the bear's heels as the crack of the rifle bullet echoed deeper than my own.

Tuukula lowered his rifle, flicked the safety switch and slung it over his shoulder as Luui clambered up the rise to take his hand. The three of us turned to look at the naked man shivering outside the hut. Tuukula squinted into the light, raised his hand to shield his eyes, before calling out to the man.

"Rassi?"

19

It took me a moment to realise I was looking at a dead man, someone who had been missing for nearly three months. But more than that, the ghostlike appearance of the naked man standing in the snow outside the broken winds of the Arctic hut, was all the more haunting because of the way he stood, rocking his weight from foot to foot, not unlike the polar bear. This man was perhaps Rassi Qisuk, but whatever connection he once had to the village of Qaanaaq, to the people and his family who lived there was gone, replaced with the husk of a body barely supporting a feral mind. Tuukula called out his name one more time, and Rassi scurried back inside the hut.

"Tuukula," I said, placing my hand on his arm as he took a step forward.

"What?"

"Be careful."

"It's Rassi."

"He was once, maybe," I said, lowering my voice. "Not anymore."

Tuukula nodded, then spoke to Luui in Greenlandic, pressing her behind his body, and, I imagined, giving her strict instructions to walk behind him, and to stay there. I walked beside them, then nodded at the spot where the polar bear had been digging. I saw Rassi's pale face at the broken window, as I led Tuukula and Luui to the pile of rocks and small rounded boulders, coated in crisp black Arctic lichen.

The polar bear had removed the first layer of rocks. I slipped my pistol inside the pouch of my smock, and then held up my hand for Tuukula to stop, shaking my head at Luui as she peered around his legs, her fingers teasing at the fur of Tuukula's trousers. I knelt by the rock pile that I could now see was a grave, removing a couple more rocks, placing them gently to one side as I revealed the grey face of a small boy. His skin, dry, like parched leather, clung to his cheekbones. The boy's teeth were small and white beneath his curled lips. The shock of black hair on his head, so thick, startled my brain into thinking that his death was recent.

"Isaja," Tuukula whispered.

I looked up as the door of the hut creaked open. Rassi stepped out, tugging a length of twine through the waist loops of his jeans and tying it over his hip as he walked towards us. He buttoned his shirt as he drew close, stopping beside Tuukula before looking at me and at the boy in the grave at my feet.

"Rassi," I said. "My name is Constable Jensen. I've been looking for Isaja."

"My boy," Rassi said, the words rasping across his tongue.

"Yes," I said. "Is this Isaja?"

Rassi nodded, once, definitive.

"What happened, Rassi?"

I stood to one side as Rassi approached the grave. I noticed his quick-bitten nails at the ends of thin fingers, and the bony cut of his shoulders protruding from his shirt as he bent down to replace the rocks. I helped him as soon as Isaja's face was covered. Then, with Luui by my side and Tuukula next to Rassi, we replaced the last of the rocks disturbed by the bear. Rassi stood up, let his hands fall limp to his sides, and then turned to walk back to the hut.

"Go," Tuukula said. "Talk to him. Luui and I will fetch food from the sledge."

"Okay," I said, as I turned to follow Rassi.

The hut was surprisingly clean, with fine snow on the windowsills instead of dust. Sheets of newspaper lined the walls, peeling at the corners. Rassi sat down on the sleeping platform. We both stared at his rifle propped against the single chair beside the table. I took the rifle and placed it outside the hut. Rassi didn't move.

I pulled the chair out from the table and sat down, curious as to how to begin. Rassi saved me the trouble, clearing his voice with a cough before he started to speak. I reached inside my smock and tugged my notebook from my shirt pocket to record his story.

"Isaja ran away," he said, in a halting but clear Danish. "A long time ago. I was angry, too angry to look for him. I thought he would come back. Maybe he had been with his *ata*. Maybe he was with Tuukula. I even thought he could be with his *anaana* in Ilulissat. The social workers could have sent him there, paid for the ticket." He looked up with lifeless eyes. "But they didn't."

"No," I said, softly. I rested my notebook in my

lap and Rassi continued.

"It took a long time for me to realise that he wasn't coming back, that it might even be my fault. I was so angry. So angry I told everybody that Aluusaq had killed my son. That he did it to spite me. But no one believed me. Then, when I stopped drinking, I heard someone talk about missing dogs. Another man said someone had stolen his sledge. No one steals sledges, maybe they borrow dogs. But what I heard made me think, and then I knew that Isaja had gone somewhere."

"You thought he came here?"

"Not at first. This was an accident. First, I went deeper into the fjord, to Qeqertat. But Isaja was not there. Then I crossed the fjord to Herbert Island. He wasn't there either. I didn't want to go to Savissivik, in the south. But I told myself I would if I didn't find him in Siorapaluk. So I sledged north," Rassi said, pausing as Tuukula and Luui entered the hut. Rassi nodded when Tuukula offered him tea. The primus spat and the ice popped and cracked as it melted in the pan. Rassi continued. "I found tracks leading up to the hut, and I followed them, but then the sledge broke through thin ice. I was so excited about the tracks; I didn't think about the ice. When the sledge started to sink, I had to cut the dogs' traces. They ran, free of the sledge, leaving me alone on the ice." Rassi looked up at Tuukula, and said, "There was nothing I could do."

"And the dogs ran to Siorapaluk," I said. "The people there thought you were dead."

"When a team arrives without a sledge, it's easy to think the driver is dead."

"But you didn't die, Rassi," Tuukula said. He poured the tea, gave Rassi a mug, adding plenty of sugar, before settling on the floor with Luui in his lap.

"I wish I had," Rassi said. "Because when I came to the hut…"

I waited for Rassi to say more, encouraging him when he didn't. "You found your son inside the hut."

Rassi nodded, pressing his palm to his bony cheek to stem the flood of tears.

"He was dead when you found him," I said. "Wasn't he?"

"He lay here," Rassi said, patting the sleeping platform. "He lay very still. He had his arms wrapped around that bloody tooth. I buried him with it, lay the tooth on top of his grave. But it is gone now. I went out hunting one day, found tracks by Isaja's grave, and the tooth was gone." Rassi swallowed, took a sip of tea, and then looked up. "Isaja must have starved to death. It was my fault."

Rassi dipped his head to his knees. The tea slopped over the lip of his mug as he sobbed. I turned at a soft scratching sound, and watched as Luui crawled off her father's lap, padded across the floor, and slipped her hands around Rassi's arm. Luui wormed her way to Rassi's chest, and I watched, brushing at my own tears trickling down my cheeks, as the tiny girl comforted her half-brother's father.

"Rassi," I said, after a few minutes of silence. "We're going to take you and Isaja home."

20

I helped Tuukula wrap Isaja's body in a tarpaulin. We carried him to a small sledge propped against the side of the hut, securing him for the journey back to Qaanaaq before pushing the sledge down to the ice. I watched as Tuukula ran a line from Isaja's sledge to his own.

"There must have been dogs. The dogs that brought Isaja and the tooth here," I said, as Tuukula finished tying his knots. "Why didn't Rassi use them to sledge back to Qaanaaq?"

"He let them go," Tuukula said.

"Why?"

"He never wanted to leave."

"But he's coming with us now. What's changed?"

Tuukula nodded at the shore where Luui helped Rassi over the ice foot.

"I told you powerful magic runs in this family. She's convinced him to come home."

I waited for Tuukula to smile, or to laugh, only to realise he was deadly serious.

"Umeerinneq told me you're a shaman. Luui said you were *angakkoq*."

"Maybe I am."

"But aren't shaman supposed to make *Tupilaq* and swim down to comb Sedna's hair?"

"So the stories say." Tuukula shrugged. "There's all kinds of magic in this world, Constable. I like to think everybody can use it."

"Like Isaja disappearing?"

"*Aap*. Exactly like that. I think, Constable," he said, "you are also a shaman."

"I doubt that," I said, with a laugh.

"You don't think so? How else did you find the boy?"

"Police work isn't magic, Tuukula."

"No? Then tell me how you found a boy who's been missing for nearly a year, when everyone else failed?"

"I asked the right people the right questions," I said. "That's all."

"*Naamik*," Tuukula said. "That's magic."

The light caught his eye as he smiled and I decided I would let him have his way, agreeing that there *might* be some magic in this world after all.

We sledged back to Qaanaaq, towing Isaja's body behind Tuukula's sledge. Rassi and Tuukula took turns to rest and drive the team. Rassi seemed to grow stronger each time he gripped the dog whip, his commands clearer and more precise with every kilometre we sledged. Luui curled up in her father's arms, pinching his nose between her finger and thumb, giggling each time he pretended to bite her. I sat quietly, content to take in the sight of the brown mountain rock, the glaciers tonguing the valleys, the pant of the dogs and the fresh tang of salt, sea and ice. I knew I would miss it, but as I slept on the sledge, I confess to thinking about a hot shower, the soft mattress of my bed, and Sunday brunch at *Katuaq*. My first missing persons case had taken me to the top of Greenland, and I had drunk deeply of the raw, wild nature and the strange magic there. But after a week, I was ready to return to the city.

I spent my last few days in Qaanaaq accompanying Umeerinneq, sleeping in the guest bedroom of the police house, and wandering the gravel streets in the late light each evening. My walks always ended by the row of small hunters' cabins looking out onto the sea, where Tuukula sat and smoked, where there was always fresh spiced tea and a hint of magic in the air.

"I'm going to miss this," I said, watching Luui chase her friends around the drying racks, as Tuukula smoked his single cigarette.

"You'll be back, one day," he said.

"Yes, I know. But I mean *this*, Tuukula. The time I spent with you and Luui."

"It sounds like you think this is the last time we'll see each other."

"Isn't it? Nuuk is a long way away, and I'll be stuck in the city most of the time."

"Stuck in the city," Tuukula said. He laughed as he finished his cigarette. "You've changed."

"No," I said. "I don't think so."

"We'll see," he said, standing up. "*And* we'll see each other again."

"Where are you going?"

"I promised Rassi that I would sit with him when he visited his father. They have a lot to talk about. I said I would help. Do you want to come?"

"In a minute," I said.

I waved at Luui, catching her eye, and beckoning her over. The dust plumed from her heels as she picked up speed, skidding to a stop as she bumped into my knees.

"Happy Birthday, Luui," I said, pressing a tube of toothpaste into her hands. Luui beamed, opening the cap as she twirled away. "Erm, that wasn't quite what I had in mind," I said, as I watched her squeeze a gob of paste onto each of her friends' fingers. Tuukula laughed as the kids thrust their fingers into their mouths, licking at the frothy paste as it bubbled over their lips.

21

The day after I arrived back in Nuuk, I noticed something odd about the surface of my desk beneath the staircase. Where there was once a single dusty box of papers there were now three. The telephone unit had been replaced with something more modern, and a call waiting light flashed red under one of the buttons.

"Don't get any grand ideas," Sergeant Duneq said, as he approached my desk. "This is a temporary assignment. You'll be back on the street and back on nights as soon as I convince the commissioner that you've still got a lot to learn. You're not…"

"Training anymore," I said, finishing the sergeant's sentence.

"What's that, Constable? Are you mocking me?"

"No, Sergeant. Not at all."

"Good." Duneq glanced at the light flashing on the phone and nodded at it. "You've got a call, Constable. I suggest you answer it."

"Yes, Sergeant."

I waited for Duneq to turn his back before I allowed myself a discreet but smug smile. Things were looking up, and the new phone, clean desk, and old files suggested that the commissioner intended to keep me busy.

"At least for a little while," I said, softly, as Duneq left the room.

I took a breath, pulled out the chair, and reached for the phone.

"Greenland Missing Persons desk," I said, as I sat down.

The chair tipped forwards, crashing into the floor as the two remaining wheels rolled backwards. If I hadn't been preoccupied breaking my fall, I might have heard the sergeant's deep guffaw from just outside the door.

Training might be over, but some things were just beginning.

The End

CONSTABLE PETRA JENSEN 1-3

Author's Note

So now you've met Tuukula and his daughter Luui. I hope you like them, because you'll meet them again – often. In the introduction, I said there was no *grand plan*, but that was perhaps a half-truth, and I hope you'll forgive me. I have *big* plans for this series of novellas, with at least twenty stories planned in my head. In my later stories, set in the far future, Petra is a police commissioner, and I am excited to explore just how she got there. *The Boy with the Narwhal Tooth* is the most recent step, but not the first.

Petra was investigating *missing persons* in my first Maratse novel: *Seven Graves, One Winter*, published on Valentine's Day in 2018. But she actually appears for the very first time in a novella called *Container*, published on December 6, 2017. So, it's not such a stretch to explore how it all began.

Will there be inconsistencies in these stories? Will Petra actually have seen and experienced more of Greenland and its culture than she lets on when meeting and falling in love with Maratse?

Sure.

But hey, everyone's got secrets.

I hope you enjoyed *The Boy with the Narwhal Tooth*. I certainly enjoyed writing it.

Chris
June 2020
Denmark

CONSTABLE PETRA JENSEN 1-3

The Girl with the Raven Tongue

Greenland Missing Persons #2

CHRISTOFFER PETERSEN

Introduction

The Girl with the Raven Tongue is another purely fictional story to which I have added generous amounts of dramatic license. The settlement of Kangaamiut does exist, but the characters and events in this story are of my own fabrication. Kangaamiut is one of the most picturesque places you can visit in Greenland.

This story is the second in a series of novellas in which we follow Constable Petra Jensen, as she investigates missing persons cases in Greenland. Each story features returning characters, and charts Petra's early career on the Greenlandic police force.

These stories are cosier than the novels featuring Petra and the dour but dependable Constable David Maratse. They are set prior to the events in the novels starting with *Seven Graves, One Winter*, and before the trilogy of Greenland thrillers of which *The Ice Star* is the first.

If you're new to my Greenland crime stories, you can read these novellas without a deeper knowledge of the semi-fictional Greenland in which they are set. You might, however, want to start with the first novella in this series: *The Boy with the Narwhal*

CONSTABLE PETRA JENSEN 1-3

Tooth.

Chris
July 2020
Denmark

CHRISTOFFER PETERSEN

1

There is something exhilarating about preparing for the Friday night shift in Greenland's capital city of Nuuk. You can see it in the faces of the officers as they prepare for the evening. I'm pretty sure the novelty will wear off quickly. But there is a camaraderie among my colleagues, a strong bond that helps all of us get through the night. Even Sergeant Kiiu "George" Duneq, with his ample stomach squeezed within the constraints of his police utility belt is quick to share a jest or jibe, something to spice up the moment, and make everyone laugh. I want to laugh along with them, but each time I try, even a creasing of my lips, Sergeant Jowls, as I call him, does his best to wipe the smile from my face.

"Training is over, Jensen."

It's his stock response, his one-liner designed to put me in my place and remind me of his, every single time. I get it. I really do. I understand I still have so much to learn, but by my reckoning one more Friday night brings me closer to that goal.

"Yes, Sergeant," I said. There was nothing else to say. There never is.

"I'm splitting you up tonight." He waddled over to where Atii Napa and I were getting ready. "You and Napa spend too much time with each other as it is."

I didn't believe that, and the look on Atii's face confirmed it. Since graduating the police academy, we had hardly seen one another, at least not as much as we would like to.

"Napa is with Sergeant Alatak tonight," Jowls said. "Jensen, you're with me."

Atii fought back a snicker until Jowls was gone, then let it out with a snort she caught in the sleeve of her jacket.

"Not fair, Atii," I said.

"You should see your face."

"You should see *yours*."

We both knew that putting Atii together with Sergeant Gaba Alatak was asking for trouble, she had been mooning over him for weeks. But for me, *another* night in the company of Sergeant Jowls, was torture, made worse by the fact that he knew it, just like he knew Atii fancied Gaba.

"We'll see each other at midnight," Atii said, slapping my arm on the way out the door.

Of course, we would, I thought, knowing that one of the bars closed at midnight, and that was likely to be the first flashpoint of the night, drawing as many officers to that location as were available. That's when I'd be bound to see Atii, but not for much more than a smile, or a nod, before we started ducking elbows and *helping* patrons on their way to the next watering hole. Some would go home; others would go to jail. It was just never clear who would end up where.

Before heading out of the office I cast one last wistful glance at my desk at the far end, tucked beneath a staircase. If the telephone rang before I started my evening shift, I would have a good excuse to postpone my patrol with Jowls. Of course, it didn't. You can't just *will* someone to disappear, at least, not that I was aware of. The phone didn't ring. I was all out of excuses, and it was time to get my butt into the car, maybe even the driving seat, although that was, generally, asking too much of Jowls. Unless he had a point to make.

The duty officer turned the volume up on the television mounted to the wall, slowing my way out of the door. We both stared at the sight of the Danish Royal Air Force Challenger jet streaking over the town of Maniitsoq, north of Nuuk, just south of the Arctic Circle. Apart from flying sovereignty missions – about which I knew next to nothing – the Challenger aircraft was used in Search and Rescue missions, when the weather, ice conditions, or geography, often all three, prevented police and volunteers from searching. The aircraft had powerful cameras that could cover large areas quickly. I had seen the footage on television and been amazed at the detail.

Of course, if the plane was flying over Maniitsoq on a Friday night in early spring, then the chances were high that someone was…

"…missing," said the duty officer. "A little girl. Last seen walking alone into the mountains."

"Alone?"

"Yep."

"How old?"

"Eleven." The duty officer, another sergeant, shook his head. "Forget it, Jensen. She's missing, but it's not an actual missing persons case. Not yet, anyway. It's too soon." He jabbed his finger towards the door. "Better get a move on. Duneq is waiting."

"I know," I said, with another glance at the television. The news camera crew from *Kalaallit Nunaata Radioa*, zoomed back to focus on the reporter as she explained the circumstances, while pointing at a distraught woman in the background of the shot. The reporter spoke in Greenlandic. I knew she would repeat it all again in Danish, but I couldn't wait, Jowls was already in the car. "Let me know what happens," I said, as I headed for the door.

"You might have a desk, Jensen," the duty officer said. "But I'm not your secretary."

I thought about saying something in return, but teasing among colleagues only went so far. I was still pretty green when it came to experience. Besides, a Friday night shift on payday was no time to let my mind wander. The little girl would have to wait. I just hoped it wouldn't be long before they found her; in the news report clip the girl's mother looked close to breaking point.

"Jensen, get a move on."

"Yes, Sergeant."

I jogged for the door, adjusting my belt, and repositioning my pistol holster over my hip, as Sergeant Duneq pointed at the driver's seat.

I almost smiled.

It had been raining since midday, and now, with a sudden drop in temperature, the conditions were perfect to test Duneq's favourite constable.

"More training," I breathed, as I opened the driver's door. "Until it's over."

I adjusted the mirrors and the seat, nodded once to Jowls, and then started the car.

The Friday night shift had begun.

2

To be fair to Sergeant Jowls, he said next to nothing about my driving. The roads were icy, as was expected, but we spent just as much time out of the car as we did inside it. Payday Fridays usually started on a Thursday and would stretch across the whole weekend, until sometime through the day on Monday. Like many residents in Nuuk, I had often been late for work because of waiting for a bus that never came on a Monday morning, the driver having enjoyed far too much of the weekend.

That Friday night, driving with Jowls, was no different.

The first call was a minor scuffle, involving just three people. We got the second call of a disturbance while driving one particularly fiery middle-aged woman to the Greenlandic equivalent of a New York drunk tank. Jowls sent me back out alone while he and the duty officer processed the woman. I sped through the less populated streets, before slowing at the junctions, and then crawling along Nuuk's main street looking for Atii and Gaba who were dealing with a fight outside Nuuk's main watering hole: *Tupilaq*, or *Tupi* as most people called it.

I felt like I was cruising for trouble as I stared through the rain-splashed windshield, peering over the wheel and squinting into the swirl of blue emergency lights reflecting off the windows of the Thai restaurant, just down the street from the bar. But then I saw Atii, as she spilled into the street with a large man clinging to her back.

The tyres of the patrol car squealed along the kerb as I turned off the engine and yanked the handbrake into position. Atii had managed to roll out from beneath the man by the time I reached her, but only just. The rain that had plastered Atii's hair to her forehead now did the same to mine, and I felt a shiver down my neck as my skin cooled in the wind. The man stumbled to his feet, reaching for Atii, until I got a grip of his wrist, bending it backwards just enough to turn the man away from the road, away from Atii, and back onto the pavement. He lashed out with his foot, and I caught the toe of his shoe on my shin, but not enough to push me off balance. Atii grabbed the man's other arm, and we *helped* him to the back of the patrol car, stuffing him into the rear while he kicked and spat.

The odour of old hops and yeast washed over us as he burped, threatening to unload the last few beers he had consumed. I risked a quick look at Atii before we pushed the man's boot inside the door and slammed it shut.

"Weren't we supposed to try and talk him down first?" I said, as Atii leaned against the rear door to catch her breath.

"I tried that, already," she said, wiping the rain from her face. "He was less than cooperative, to put it mildly."

"And where's Gaba?"

Atii pointed up the street. "Outside *Tupi*. With everyone else. This one," she said, tapping her finger on the glass of the door, "decided to make a run for it. I would have let him go, but Gaba told me to go get him. Something about him being a repeat offender, and the fact that he started the fight at the bar."

"So, you decided to impress Gaba, eh?"

"Don't start, P," Atii said, waving her finger.

She had that look, the one with the single arched eyebrow. I had teased her many times about how her eyebrow was hooked to the corner of her mouth, scrunching her nose as her mouth stretched to the right. It was a difficult look to mimic, but I tried my best, and nine times out of ten, it made Atii smile. But maybe she was tired that night, or I had hit a little too close to home. Regardless, the look that I loved so much faded as she nodded back up the street.

"We'd better get going," she said.

"Shall I take this one back to the station?"

I was getting used to the taxi run. Besides, not speaking Greenlandic had its advantages on Friday nights. I was often the designated driver, and I didn't mind the monotony of driving to the station and back.

"Sure," Atii said. "I'll see you in a while."

I watched her walk a short distance up the hill before climbing in behind the wheel. The drunk in the back was quieter than he had been on the street, and he changed tack as I started the car.

"I'm not a bad man, really," he said, switching

to Danish when he realised I didn't grasp Greenlandic.

"I understand," I said, as I pulled away from the kerb.

"You can let me go. I'm calm now."

"I'm sure you are."

It was a classic response, as if the trip to the station sobered some, though by no means all, of the Friday night drunks into startling moments of clarity. And some inspired ingenuity when searching for a way to avoid a night in jail.

"I could give you information," the man said. "I know things. And, if I told you them, you could let me go."

"It doesn't work like that," I said, as I turned down the street leading to the station.

The man fell silent, and I thought he had given up, but I soon discovered that he was wracking his beer-addled brain for just the right titbit of information that might get him out of the boot of my patrol car.

"I could tell you about the girl," he said. "The one they're looking for in the mountains."

I have to admit I slowed the car when he said that, parking on the side of the road before twisting the rear-view mirror to get a better look at him.

"Her name is Iiva Suersaq," he said. "And I know all about her."

3

"You're not working a missing persons case," Jowls said, pointing at the drunk from my car as the man slumped in a plastic chair beside the duty officer's desk. "It's Friday night, Jensen. Did you forget? Or is your ego so big now that you think stopping fights on the street is beneath you?"

"That's not what I think," I said, "But they're still looking for her." I pointed at the television screen on the wall. "If he knows something about her..."

"We'll pass it on. When we have time, Constable Jensen." Jowls stabbed his finger at the door, and said, "You're needed back on the street."

I thought of several responses, but bit my tongue, hard enough to taste blood, and then stormed out of the station, back into the rain.

Jowls wasn't wrong, but I knew that the idea of a lowly constable having a desk and a phone gnawed at him. I was supposed to be fresh out of the academy – which I was. But *my* understanding of police work included using a high degree of initiative. We were supposed to think and consider our actions, *before* acting. Sometimes we had to think fast. But it seemed to me that every time *I* started to think, Duneq was there to put me in my place.

Of course, it could have been jealousy. Like many close-knit cultures, we Greenlanders were not immune to that. It could also have been because I was a woman, younger than him, at the very start of my career. I opened the patrol car door, frowning as a sympathetic thought fractured my mood. I batted the thought away – I wasn't ready to take Sergeant Duneq's side, or to see it from his perspective. Slamming the door helped. As did throwing the police car into gear, roaring out of the parking lot, and spinning into the street.

I was too focused on trying to remain angry to notice the black skin of ice lining the road.

The minute I left the gravel surface of the police parking lot, the rear end of the patrol car settled onto the ice, spinning me around until I was facing the police station. The passenger side of the car bounced over the sand and grit lining the side of the road, catching me by surprise, and flooding my body with adrenalin, as I thought about the irrigation ditch running alongside the road. I'd like to say it was experience, or more of that quick thinking I was convinced a young police constable such as myself was capable of. Whatever it was guiding my foot to the accelerator, stomping on the pedal as I wrenched the steering wheel down to the left, it smelled a lot like luck to me. I hit the brakes as I pulled away from the ditch, skidding to a stop with one set of wheels on the grit and the other on the slick asphalt.

"Stupid," I said, casting a glance at the police station to see if anyone was watching.

I saw Sergeant Duneq leaning against the wall

CONSTABLE PETRA JENSEN 1-3

beside the front door, his arms wrapped around his belly as he tucked fat thumbs into his low-hanging utility belt. The light from the entrance was strong enough to reveal the sneer on his face, and I could just imagine his voice, reminding me that *training was over.*

I wondered if it ever would be, and if that really was the point of it all, that we were always learning, that no two days were alike.

I checked the mirrors, breathed a sigh of relief that the only thing that had taken a hit was my pride, and then pulled away, turning slowly in the street. I headed back to the centre of Nuuk, cruising the streets for customers too rowdy for the average taxi. It didn't take long to find them, and I spent another two hours shuttling back and forth from the street to the station.

Back at the station, Jowls didn't say anything. Nor did he react as I checked the duty officer's list of guests in the cells, noting that Ulaajuk Corneliussen, my second customer that evening, was in cell three.

4

Ulaajuk Corneliussen's story was similar to that of the men and women in the cells either side of him. Armed with little more than a superficial education, plagued by truancy – his own and his teachers', Ulaajuk had once clung to the belief that he could make a living as his father did, hunting and fishing. But when the reality of life in the concrete apartment blocks of Nuuk struck him, when it became clear that fishing and hunting for a living was little more than a sentimental dream, Ulaajuk found his escape in alcohol.

As sad as it was, there were so many Ulaajuks in Greenland, they created a stereotype that foreigners, and especially Danes, with that strange mix of post-colonial affection and disdain, found all too easy to believe. I knew that we had the same potential as the Danes and the Europeans among us, but that circumstance often prevented us from achieving the goals we set in our youth. Changing course required more than just willpower; a helping hand was often necessary, just to hold certain doors open, long enough to allow people like Ulaajuk to step through them.

And people like me, I thought, as I unlocked Ulaajuk's door.

The few hours' rest, some food and coffee, had

given Ulaajuk time to sober up. Enough, I hoped, to jog his memory about the girl. He stirred as I entered the cell, swinging his legs over the side of the bed as I sat down on the chair opposite him.

"You're staying the night," I said, as he looked up. "I'm not here to let you go."

"Okay," he said. He brushed his thick black fringe out of his eyes.

"I'm on a break. But I want to know about the girl."

"Iiva?"

"Yes."

Ulaajuk nodded. "She's a good girl. I hope they find her."

"You said you could tell me about her. Maybe what you tell me will help."

I resisted the urge to wrinkle my nose as Ulaajuk shifted on the bed. He might have sobered up, but the confines of the cell did nothing to dampen the heady mix of fart, beer and sweat. Ulaajuk rested his hands in his lap. With his legs stretched out on the bed, and his back against the wall, he reminded me of a hunter on his sledge, perhaps even a younger Tuukula. The thought made me smile, and I wondered what Tuukula and Luui would have said about my wild ride out of the parking lot. Ulaajuk brought me back to the present with a soft cough as he cleared his throat to speak.

"They say she has a raven tongue," he said, as I tugged my notebook out of my jacket pocket.

"Why?"

"Hair lip," Ulaajuk said, tapping his top lip. "She sounds funny when she speaks. The other children tease her."

"Funny?" I fought back a sudden wave of pity for Iiva. With my limited Greenlandic, I knew what it was like to have something children could make fun of. But pity wouldn't help me find her, when or perhaps *if* I was even given the chance.

"*Aap*." Ulaajuk nodded. "It sounds like she speaks through her nose."

"Then why do they say she has a raven tongue?"

"Because she can talk like a raven – every sound."

I made a note, pausing with my pen on the paper as I thought about the range of raven calls that I had heard over the years. Such noisy brutes, they are so entangled in our daily lives it's difficult to imagine a Greenland without ravens. For the same reason, it can be difficult to think about them in a more abstract way. But as Ulaajuk told me about Iiva, I remembered my own childhood, how we used to try and mimic the ravens, calling them to us, only to have them dance away as we tried to catch them.

"Iiva found a raven nest once," Ulaajuk said. "She was five. The adults were gone, and she looked after the young." He scratched his head. "Two, I think."

"She reared them?"

"What?"

"She fed them," I said.

"*Aap*."

"And they followed her around?"

"All over town." The dim light from the cell

lamp in the ceiling danced across Ulaajuk's dark brown eyes as if he was remembering another story about Iiva Suersaq and her ravens. "They used to sit on the school roof, opposite her class," he said, straightening his arm and shaping his hand like a beak.

He tucked one hand under his elbow, splaying his fingers like claws, and I imagined them gripping the edge of a roof. The memory of ravens hopping and scratching the bitumen roofs at the children's home brought a smile to my face as Ulaajuk continued.

"The teachers would send her out to shoo them away. But then she never came back. She would spend all day with them." The light in Ulaajuk's eyes faded as the raven evaporated. He returned his hands to his lap. "Her father, her *ataata*, hated the ravens."

"Why?"

"He wanted her to make friends, and to stay in school. He didn't believe the ravens could teach her anything." Ulaajuk dipped his head, resting his chin on his chest.

"Ulaajuk," I said. "How do you know Iiva?"

The light flickered as Ulaajuk looked up. I had the strangest feeling that he was drawing on the energy from the lamp, just as the light had made his eyes dance, now it seemed to lift him, giving him courage to say something – perhaps even to confess.

I waited for him to speak, lowering my notepad to my thigh. The chair creaked in the sudden silence of the cell.

"Iiva is my niece, my sister's daughter. I used

to look after her when I lived in Maniitsoq. Before I moved to Nuuk." The light flickered, surging, released from Ulaajuk's grasp.

"You think it's your fault that she ran away?"

I bit my lip as soon as I said it, wishing I had kept the thought to myself, wondering if I was fishing for a confession, as I imagined all kinds of scenarios where an uncle might have abused the trust of his sister, and taken advantage of Iiva. There was, unfortunately, plenty of documentation and many cases to support such a theory. But as I waited for Ulaajuk to respond, I realised there were just as many alternatives.

"*Aap*," he said, lifting his head. "I let her down."

"How?"

"Before I moved to Nuuk – a few years ago – she used to talk to me when her *anaana* was working, and she couldn't talk to her *ataata*."

"Why couldn't she talk to her father?"

Ulaajuk took a breath, and then said, "Because he hates ravens."

5

"My dad's friend had a hair lip," Atii said, in my apartment after our shift had ended. She slumped in the chair opposite mine at the kitchen table. Breakfast, she had decided, should be at my place, and we agreed that everything in the fridge or the cupboards should be fried. It's amazing how the palate craves fat after working long dark hours, at least, that's what we told ourselves. After ploughing through fried bread, fried bacon and experimental granola – cornflakes not oats, there was little left to do but finish our coffee before crashing on the sofa with an episode or two of something, *anything*, before we returned to the station for the Saturday evening shift.

I reached over the table to twist a strand of Atii's hair out of her coffee and was rewarded with a tired smile, followed by a long sigh.

"He had surgery when he was a kid, but he still talked funny," she said. And then, "I think they call it a *cleft* lip now."

"And people need surgery?"

"*Aap*," she said. "I'm pretty sure. Something about eating, breathing, and talking. All of which is difficult with a hole in your palate." Atii paused to stick her finger in her mouth, frowning as she poked around the roof of her mouth. "God, I'm tired," she said, wiping her finger on her trousers. "What are we watching?"

"*Friends* or…"

"*Friends*," Atii said. "That's about all I can manage."

I finished my coffee as Atii drifted from the kitchen to the sofa. The cushions sighed as she flopped onto them. She hooked one stockinged foot over the back of the sofa as she rummaged around for the remote.

"On the coffee table," I said, as my phone rang.

"Tell them you're not home," Atii said. She flicked the television on, then reached for the second remote to turn on the DVD player.

"It's Jowls," I said, suppressing a sigh as I answered my phone.

My sympathetic gene, the one I suppressed earlier in my shift, engaged as I listened to Sergeant Duneq. He sounded even more tired than Atii. But as soon as I realised the direction in which the call was heading, I wished I'd never answered it.

"What?" Atii said, as I stuffed my phone into my pocket. She muted the *Friends* introduction and waited for me to speak.

"He wants me to go in."

"Now? You've only just got off."

"Someone called in sick."

"So? You've just done a night shift."

"He said there's no one else."

"Then let *him* do it."

As tempting as it was, I knew I would go in. My mind was already in the hall, waiting for my body to catch up, to slip into my jacket and pull on my boots.

"It's just a few hours. He's got someone coming in at noon."

"Noon? What about our morning together?"

"You'll be asleep before the opening credits," I said, tucking my hair behind my ear as I nodded at the television. "You always are."

"That's hardly the point, P."

"I know, but that's the way it is." I leaned over the back of the sofa to kiss Atii's head, then plucked the remote from her hand to toss it onto the armchair by the balcony door. "If you want sound..." I said, waiting for a response.

Atii rolled onto her side, hugging the pillow to her chest as she settled into the sofa. "I've seen this one before."

"Atii," I said, as I walked down the short corridor to the front door. "We've seen them *all* before."

"Right."

"I'll catch you later."

"At noon?"

"*Imaqa*. Maybe. Gaba has invited me to lunch."

"What?" I paused, fingers clasped around my jacket zip. "You never said."

"You never asked."

"I guess I didn't."

I shouted goodbye as I left my apartment, wishing her luck and reminding her to behave. I waited for a response before closing my door, but all I could hear were Atii's soft snores drifting down the hall.

Jowls sent a patrol car to pick me up, making

me think he wasn't all bad, and I clambered into the passenger seat. Constable Kuno Schmidt grinned as he pressed a cup of takeaway coffee into my hands.

"Thought you might need this," he said, as I settled into my seat.

"You're a lifesaver, Kuno."

"You say that now but wait 'til we get to the station."

"What's going on?"

"Duneq is all fired up over something."

"Something about me?"

"You could say that." Kuno braked for a stop sign, resting his elbow on the side of the door, and tapping his fingers against his bald head. From a certain angle he reminded me of Gaba, and I wondered if Kuno was losing his hair, or borrowing the look from the SRU leader. He accelerated once the traffic started to move, then slowed for a bus to pull away from the kerb. The rain glistened on the granite lumps that rose like black pyramids behind the new high rises lining the road out of Qinngorput. "It's your phone," he said, as he settled in behind the bus. "It's been ringing all morning."

"My phone?" I said, blinking my way out of drowsiness and back into the conversation.

"The one on the missing persons desk."

"It's ringing?"

"Yes," Schmidt said. He turned his head to smile. "You really are tired, aren't you?"

"Yes," I said. But the prospect of a missing persons case lit a small fire in my belly, and I felt its glow spread through my body. "I'll need more coffee," I said, and Schmidt nodded.

CONSTABLE PETRA JENSEN 1-3

6

Sergeant Duneq was sitting on one end of my desk, looking just as tired as I felt, if not more so. His arms were folded stiffly on top of his stomach, as he scowled at Commissioner Lars Andersen. He turned his scowl towards me as I walked along one side of the long open office to the stairs at the far end. The Greenland missing persons desk – *my* desk – was stuffed beneath the stairs, in an area that Jowls dared me to call an office.

"I appreciate your concern," the commissioner said, nodding at me as I approached. "But this is a matter of national interest. It's already all over the news. The military need the Challenger jet on the east coast, and the politicians are claiming that we have given up the search. But the fact is, we have exhausted the possibilities. We have to show that we haven't given up, even after the search has been called off."

I caught a flash of something in the sergeant's eyes at the word *search*, and then the fuzziness of a late night shift, followed by an extra morning at work, cleared. Suddenly I realised they were talking about the missing girl.

"You mean they've stopped looking for Iiva Suersaq?" I said, drawing a look of wrath from Jowls, and a much softer and curious response from the commissioner.

"What do you know about her?" the commissioner asked.

"Only that she's eleven. She's been teased a lot – probably."

"Teased?"

"She has a cleft lip, and…" I paused, trying to remember what Atii had said. "A cleft palate – I think the two go together. Something that would make it hard for her to fit in." I was back in familiar territory and waking up, encouraged by the commissioner's nods of approval. "That might be a reason why she got lost in the first place," I said.

"You don't know that, Constable."

Jowls fixed me with a hard stare, raising his eyebrows, as if ordering me to stand down. But with the police commissioner standing right beside us, I was too excited to stand down. It was probably one of the reasons Sergeant Duneq made my life as miserable as possible. *Enthusiasm,* he had once told me, *was for intellectuals. But police work is practical work, Jensen. Remember that.*

I did remember. I remembered everything Jowls told me, if only to prove him wrong, every chance I got.

"Let her finish, George," the commissioner said.

Andersen took a more casual stance, resting his arm on top of a tall filing cabinet before gesturing for me to continue. I wasn't short, but the more time I spent with the commissioner, the shorter he made me feel. I took a breath, avoiding Jowls' renewed attempts to stare me into submission, and continued.

"If they've called off the search," I said, thinking on the spot. "That might suggest she's not lost but hiding."

"Or dead," Jowls said.

"I appreciate your optimism, Constable," the commissioner said, with a glare at Jowls. "But we're assuming the worst. It has been a wet and cold weekend. Plenty of ice in the foothills, more in the mountains. But," he said, with a wave of his hand. "Keep going. Elaborate."

"Okay," I said. "Supposing she's alive, then she might have a preferred hiding place, somewhere she's been before. It might be high up – higher than expected."

My desk creaked as Jowls shifted his weight. A deep crease of something like curiosity furrowed his brow as he leaned forwards. "What makes you say that?"

I shelved the realisation that he was curious, saving that thought for another time, as I scrabbled for an explanation.

"Because of the ravens," I said.

"Ravens?"

It was the commissioner's turn to frown.

"Yes. Her uncle told me she reared some orphan ravens."

"Orphan ravens?" Jowls snorted, and I paused, waiting for him to crack a comment about my orphan childhood. To his credit, and to my amazement, he didn't. Which only put me even more on the spot, as I searched for an explanation.

"She's been teased," I said.

Jowls snorted for a second time. "You've said

that already."

"Yes…"

"Go on, Constable," the commissioner said. "Never mind the sergeant. Tell me about the ravens and the girl's uncle."

"Her uncle, Ulaajuk, is in the cell downstairs."

"Was," Jowls said. "I let him go this morning."

"But before he went," I said, suppressing a sudden rush of urgency, and the thought that I might need to interview the girl's uncle again. "He said that Iiva spent lots of time with the ravens. They followed her around, and people shunned her even more because of that. Her cleft lip would have left a scar, and maybe a speech difficulty. It would have made her an easy target. Add the ravens to that and…" I paused as the duty officer knocked on the office door.

"Sergeant?" he said. "Can I have a word?"

The commissioner waited for Jowls to leave, then lifted his finger for me to hold any further thoughts I might have.

"The media is involved now, asking all kinds of questions about budgets and resources," he said, once Duneq and the duty officer had left the office. "Which means the politicians are obliged to comment. Now, I don't know much about the situation, only the basics. You've already told me more than I think anyone involved in the search knows. Which is why I'm sending you to Kangaamiut."

"Kangaamiut?"

"The village where Iiva Suersaq lives. Apparently, it was the old trading station, way back when, before they resettled in Maniitsoq." The commissioner laughed. "That's enough history for now."

"You're sending me today?" I barely heard the last part of what the commissioner said about history.

"Yes," he said, with a nod of his head. "I know you're tired, Constable."

I was, and yet, surprisingly, I was gaining strength as he spoke.

"I'm all right."

"Well," the commissioner smiled. "Let's pretend that you are. But let me make this clear. You will be seen as little more than a gesture. The family – the media too – will be expecting a renewed search. We simply don't have the resources, and the Challenger jet is unavailable. Between you and me, if the Challenger couldn't find her or even her body…"

"She might not want to be found," I said.

"Right. Which lends a little more credence to your theory. But, regardless of all that, this search, and this girl, suddenly got politicised. But nothing changes the fact that someone told the girl's mother that we now have a dedicated missing persons desk, and she called to ask for your help. Not by name," the commissioner said, as I started to speak. "But she might as well have. So, I'm sending you up the coast to look for Iiva. But I want you to understand that she is probably dead, and that really, your main task, is to confirm that, so we can close the case and allow the girl's parents to grieve." The commissioner paused for a second, dipping his head to look in my eyes. "Do you understand, Constable?"

"Yes."

"Good." He took a breath. "Now, with the limited resources available, and some funds I can scrape together, tell me what you think you might need. Bear in mind I can't give you any staff. I think Sergeant Duneq would have a stroke if I did," he said, and laughed.

"Yes, Sir," I said, as I thought about the girl, the reason she might be hiding, not lost. I thought about the ravens, and how she might be closer to nature than I was, and how the other children and adults shunned her for her strangeness. If she talked with the ravens, they might even think she had magical powers.

It was the thought of magic that did it.

"I do need some help," I said.

"And I said I can't spare any more officers."

"I know," I said. "But Tuukula isn't a police officer. He's a shaman."

7

I rested my arms on the table in the airport waiting lounge in Nuuk, as I left a message on Atii's phone, wishing her luck with Gaba, before smiling at our different weekend *dates*. While Atii would be trying to keep her cool while staring at the muscle-bound Sergeant Alatak, leader of the Special Response Unit, with his shaved and oiled head and perfect pectorals... I had to stop myself at that point, as I found the image of Gaba's chest more than a little distracting. *Let Atii be distracted,* I thought, as a smile crept across my lips. I would be spending the rest of the weekend, and maybe longer, with a seventy-year-old magician and his five-year-old daughter. If I avoided all further thoughts of Gaba Alatak, and what he might be doing with my best friend, I found the anticipation of seeing Tuukula and Luui again to be more than compensation.

"Gaba invited Atii," I whispered to myself, as they called my flight. "Not me."

I tugged my daypack onto my shoulder as I stood up, slipped my phone inside my jacket pocket, and got in line for the flight. The passengers disembarked, filing down the steps of the De Havilland Dash 7, which was parked on the apron outside the lounge. I caught the familiar blue-black uniform of a police officer as he followed the other passengers to the baggage area, but no matter how hard I tried, I couldn't place him. It was silly to think that I could possibly know all the police officers in Greenland, but we were a relatively small group, supported by temporary officers from Denmark, like Kuno Schmidt. Although, in Kuno's case, it was widely known that he was choosing longer and longer temporary positions. It was just a matter of time before he applied for a permanent one. But the police officer walking into the airport was new to me.

The passengers in front of me shuffled forwards as the door ahead of us opened. We filed into the baggage area, before showing our boarding cards at the gate. I caught the police officer's eye, and he grunted in return. The grunt did little to invite further conversation, and I let him be. Although, his deep brown skin, wispy oriental-style beard, and keen eyes intrigued me. He looked like he spent a lot of time outdoors. That thought brought me sharply back into the moment, and I sloughed off another bout of tiredness as I walked to the Dash 7, climbing on-board with no more thoughts about the police officer in the airport. The plane took off according to schedule, and I made myself comfortable, hoping to catch at least an hour's sleep between take-off and landing. When Jowls heard about my assignment and my final destination of Kangaamiut, he let a smile cross his face as he showed me the weather forecast on his phone just before I left the station, highlighting the strong winds with gleeful taps of his pudgy fingers.

"You'd better sleep on the flight, Jensen," he

had said. "Because the boat ride is going to be rough."

Maybe Jowls was right, but it didn't make any difference. I couldn't sleep, my brain was too awake for that. So, I said *yes* to coffee with plenty of sugar and cream. I made space for my cup on the table alongside my notebook and smartphone. Between texting Atii and checking my flight, I had time to find out more about cleft lips and palates, marking notes on my phone, before adding them to my notebook. I tucked my hair behind my ear as I worked, sucking at my top lip as I tried to imagine what services would be available to a family with a small child in need of speech therapy. *There would be something in Maniitsoq,* I thought, but I knew that the search had been in Kangaamiut, the mountainous coastal settlement where the girl lived. Getting to and from the town would be prohibitive enough, even in good weather, making it difficult to keep regular appointments.

The captain announced that we would be landing, adding a courteous reminder about the turbulence often encountered when landing in Maniitsoq – something about a right-angle turn on the approach. I stuffed my notebook and phone into my pockets, finished my coffee and readied myself for a bumpy landing.

The captain wasn't wrong. There was plenty of turbulence to make the approach to Maniitsoq *interesting*. But the turbulent landing was gentle, compared to Luui's welcome hug as she launched herself from Tuukula's arms and into mine.

"I've missed you too," I said, as Luui pressed

her face into my neck, and stuffed her cold fingers into the collar of my jacket. I stepped to one side to let the other passengers weave around me, the shaman, and his daughter.

"You're lucky we were close," Tuukula said.

"Where were you?"

"Visiting Luui's mother in Ilulissat." Tuukula smiled as a mischievous light flashed in his eyes. "So," he said, avoiding any further comment. "We are looking for a missing girl?"

"Yes," I said, tilting my head to one side as Luui played with my ponytail. "But we have to keep it quiet. That's why it's just you, me and Luui."

"We need to keep it quiet?" Tuukula frowned, and I smiled as his bushy grey eyebrows arced in thick curves beneath his thick grey hair. He wore the same tight bun on top of his head that I remembered from the first time we met in the far north of Greenland.

"It's complicated and political," I said, as Luui and I rubbed noses. She squirmed in my arms and I set her down, curious at how much she had grown in such a short space of time. "No media, so no interviews. We're here to help the family, and find the girl, as quietly as possible."

Tuukula dipped his head towards the door leading out of the airport and into a car park full of cars, as well as a small crowd of journalists and photographers.

It occurred to me that very few people knew I was going to Kangaamiut. I wondered who might have tipped off the press and immediately I thought of Jowls. It would be just like him to complicate things, even when we were supposed to be on the same side.

"Okay. This just got interesting."

8

Unlike Denmark or other countries with a road or rail infrastructure, or cheaper and more regular flights, journalists' movements in Greenland are limited. Here there would often be a local representative of Greenland's national television and radio station *Kalaallit Nunaata Radioa*, ready to drop what they were doing to follow a story. Local journalists might be teachers, shopkeepers or postal workers, anyone with an interest in the news, or simply the best available person in the right place at the right time. The journalists waiting in a small gaggle outside the airport building in Maniitsoq fit all categories, including professional journalists from *Sermitsiaq* and one Danish newspaper. I stalled at the door, taking a breath as I wondered how best to navigate through the throng to the police patrol car idling at the far end of the parking area.

"Here," Tuukula said, as he lifted Luui into my arms. "I'll deal with this."

Luui said something in the Qaanaaq dialect of Greenlandic, and Tuukula responded with a soft brush of his lips on her cheek and a whisper in her ear.

"What did she say?" I asked.

"That she can walk. That she's not a baby

anymore." Tuukula shrugged. "I told her I agreed, but that you needed a cuddle. In which case, she said you could carry her all the way to the boat."

I had forgotten about the boat, but the thought of carrying Luui *all* the way made my arms sag before Tuukula had even opened the door. Luui wrapped her thin arms around my neck and I shifted my grip to support her bottom; her feet slapped at the sides of my backpack, as she wormed her toes into the straps as if they were stirrups. Tuukula opened the door and led the way.

It might have been a small group of journalists, but they were tenacious, reflecting the local and national interest in the fate of the missing girl, and the reasons why the search had been called off. I dodged one microphone, and then slipped behind Tuukula. I blinked once in the flash of a camera, and then paused as Tuukula seemed to grow taller, right in front of me.

"Magic," Luui whispered in my ear, fiddling her tongue around the English word.

I was taller than Tuukula. I mean I *was* taller than him. But without a word, in any language, Tuukula seemed to anticipate each of the journalists' steps, as if he knew where they were going before they did. When a woman tried to take a picture, Tuukula appeared in front of her, a beat before she lifted the camera. More than one journalist poked a microphone into his chest, then pulled back with an apology on their lips, as if they were suddenly struggling with spatial relations. It made me think of public *relations*, and how refreshing it would be to be able to dodge difficult questions. But Tuukula didn't dodge anything, he *anticipated* movement, and he did so all the way to the patrol car, parting the journalists and clearing a path.

"I'm sorry," the local constable said, as he opened the rear passenger door. "I thought it best to wait by the car."

"It's okay," I said, as Luui tumbled out of my arms and onto the back seat. I glanced at Tuukula, now normal size, as he walked around the car to get in the back beside his daughter.

"Jiihu Eliassen," the constable said, thrusting his hand forwards to greet me. He wore a lopsided grin beneath a thin moustache. "I'm to take you straight to the boat."

"I thought I might get briefed at the station," I said.

"No time. Not if you want to make the boat. Otherwise you have to wait three more days before you can sail to Kangaamiut." Eliassen grinned as he backed out of the parking space. "But it's going to be bumpy. Big waves today."

I looked out at the deep blue sea and the white caps crashing into and around the icebergs plying the waters off Maniitsoq.

"Tell me about the search," I said, as Eliassen pulled away from the airport.

"We searched for two days, on foot. We had the Challenger for a few hours on the second day." He poked his finger towards the roof, and I resisted the urge to look upwards. "We found nothing, and the Challenger saw nothing. Nothing on thermal. No heat signatures. Nothing."

"So, no body?" I said, lowering my voice as I caught a glimpse of Luui in the backseat, teasing her father with spider fingers crawling on his legs.

"Unless she drowned," Eliassen said, also whispering. "We should have found a trace of something, but all we found was a pair of her shoes."

"Shoes?"

"Sneakers – dirty and patched."

"And they were the shoes she was wearing, when she disappeared?"

"Ah, *that* I don't know," Eliassen said. He slowed to let a small delivery truck drive past before entering the docks and driving all the way to the boat's gangplank. He stopped the car and turned the engine off. Sea spray pattered the window as the car rocked gently in the wind. "The mother, Kilaala Suersaq, hasn't said much. She's too upset."

"And the father?"

"Saamoq? He hasn't said anything. But we had a call early this morning. He was seen going into the mountains. The neighbour said it looked like he was going hunting."

"He took a rifle?" Tuukula asked.

"*Aap.*"

Tuukula nodded once, and then settled back on the seat. Eliassen watched him for a moment, glanced at me, and then asked, "Are you some kind of consultant? A tracker, maybe?"

"*Naamik*," Tuukula said. "I am *angakkoq*, a shaman."

"Right…" Eliassen nodded his head, slowly.

"Tuukula has helped me before," I said. "We

found a missing boy in Qaanaaq."

"And the girl?" Eliassen asked. "Shouldn't she be in school?"

"Luui is five years old," Tuukula said. "I'm home-schooling her."

"To be a shaman?" Eliassen suppressed a laugh.

Tuukula shook his head. "*Naamik*. Luui is already a shaman. I'm teaching her to be a good one."

I jumped at the sudden blast of the boat horn, recognising my cue to catch the boat before the conversation really started to get interesting.

"We have to go," I said, opening my door.

The wind curled around the edges, tugging the door out of my grasp, until I took a firmer grip of the handle. Luui hopped out of the car on the lee side of the wind, flapping her arms like wings as Tuukula grabbed a canvas holdall from the rear of the police car. I didn't remember him carrying it from the airport, and wondered if it was more magic, if he could just conjure things at will.

"I arrived early," he said, as I stared at the bag. "I met the constable then. He said he was waiting for you." Tuukula grinned and then nodded at the large blue-hulled boat. The ice-class passenger ferry was well-suited to Greenland's coastal waters, providing a lifeline for Greenlanders for whom the cost of flying was prohibitive. "But we shouldn't wait any longer."

"No," I said, as I looked at the gangplank. It shuddered in the wind. I rarely ever got seasick, but then I rarely ever sailed. I just hoped Tuukula had some kind of magic for nausea. I tucked the thought away for later as I followed the shaman and his daughter onto the boat to Kangaamiut.

9

I divided my time on the boat between freezing on deck and warming up inside until the need to vomit sent me back to the railings. Tuukula, as I expected, weathered the storm better than most of the passengers, but spent his time looking after his two girls, as he now called us. I drank a little of the bottled water he gave me, and then more as he watched me, waiting for me to take more than just a swallow.

"It's just going to come back up anyway," I said, shouting into the wind between bouts of nausea.

The bow of the boat crashed into another wave, before dipping the port side into the quarter hatched sea, only to roll back to starboard. Luui clung to her father's chest, her little face squished into his shoulder as he whipped a cotton smock from his holdall into a makeshift harness, binding his daughter to his chest. He fished a bandana out of his pocket, and I wondered if he was going to attach himself to me, perhaps tying our wrists together with cotton handcuffs.

"For your mouth," he said, pressing the bandana into my hand.

Luui wretched, and Tuukula turned his back towards the railing, as Luui spilled the little she had left in her stomach over the railings, splashing a thin stream down her father's back.

"Two hours," Tuukula said to me, as he wiped Luui's mouth.

I didn't think I could last two minutes.

But, in a moment of calm, when the crazy path of the waves aligned and everything was still, if only for a second, I saw a beauty in the blue-black sea. There was something reassuring in its power. When I looked at the obsidian surface, it looked back – not a reflection, but deeper somehow, as if there were secrets below, waiting to be revealed at the right time, to the right people, but not until they were ready to comprehend them. I had little doubt that Tuukula knew many of the secrets of the deep, and that he was teaching Luui the easier ones already. But it seemed to me, in my nauseous state, that I was paying the price for urgency, in an effort to get to Kangaamiut as quickly as possible, when I should have waited for better weather.

In Greenland you are at the mercy of the waves, the wind, and the ice and sometimes it pays to wait, and in the waiting, wisdom is often revealed. But for the life of me, I couldn't fathom what wisdom I would find staring over the side of the boat into the black sea.

And then the wind picked up.

I grasped the rail and heaved once more, and, together, Luui and I splashed Tuukula's clothes, as he took care of us.

I lost track of time, but as the sun broke through the anvil clouds above, and the waves leaked their energy back into the sea, the village of Kangaamiut, with its red, and green and blue wooden houses, popped out of the brown and black granite mountains. The peaks were slick with rain, shrouded in mist, now sparkling with rainbow orbs caught in the sun's rays. The boat slowed and the engines settled into a steady rumble, pushing us forwards until the dock loomed and the passengers began to gather their things.

"Kangaamiut," Tuukula said, as he unwrapped Luui from his chest.

"We made it," I said.

Luui slid down her father's leg as he lowered her to the deck. She clung to his knee, resting her head on his thigh as the crew moored the boat alongside the dock. The wind played with Luui's hair, tickling her face with long black strands. I could feel it doing the same with my hair, and I stared through a swathe of loose black strands, too tired to tuck them away.

There was a small group of people on the dock, huddled like the journalists, but with a patient energy that suggested they had been waiting a long time, that they would wait even longer, if need be. I watched the group – all women – as the crew rattled the gangplank into position and we prepared to disembark. Tuukula gestured for me to go on ahead, and as I walked down the gangplank, the group of women shuffled towards it, breaking the tiny circle to reveal another woman within. Never had I seen a more fragile soul, and, when she took my hands, her fragility seeped into my pores and I pulled her into my arms.

"My name is Petra," I said. "I've come to find

your daughter."

10

Even though I am a part of Greenland and Greenland is a part of me, I am constantly reminded that it is the simple things that can have the greatest impact on people's lives. Perhaps it is the nature of life in Greenland. Even with the comforts that modern life provides, we are still living on borrowed land. Not borrowed from another people, but borrowed from nature, from the elements, at the mercy and whim of all those forces we simply can't control. We don't even try. It will be the visitors you see at the airport desk asking about the delayed flight, while the Greenlanders simply look out of the window, checking the weather, before returning to their iPads, their phones or just waiting, quietly, patiently.

Kilaala Suersaq had been waiting for word of her daughter for two long days. Hers was a forced patience. Helped and supported by her family and friends, Kilaala could do nothing but wait. And judging by the looks of her straggled hair, her bloodshot eyes, and the sniff that could have been a summer cold, but wasn't, Kilaala's patience had taken a toll on her mind and her body.

I was, perhaps, too quick to say I had come to find her daughter, and a quick glance at Tuukula confirmed it. But the act of coming to Kangaamiut, of making the effort – even though it was my job – seemed to lift her a little, and my words tumbled out before I could think through the consequences.

"I'll find her," I said, as Kilaala squeezed me so tightly I struggled for breath.

It was Luui who came to my rescue, plucking at Kilaala's jeans, waiting to be introduced. Even at five years old, it seemed that the shaman's daughter understood people. She understood what they needed. Kilaala's tears welled out of her eyes as she bent down to greet Luui, taking the little girl in her arms, as Tuukula introduced himself to Kilaala's friends. I caught the names but struggled with the comments they made in Greenlandic. Tuukula whispered a translation as Kilaala took Luui's hand and led us back along the dock and into the village.

"It's been tough," he said. "The women told me that Kilaala has not slept, that she can't sleep. Not until Iiva comes home."

"I said I would find her, Tuukula."

"*Aap.*"

"I spoke too soon. What if we can't find her?"

The probability of succeeding where a coordinated search from the land and the air had failed, was slim, but the commissioner believed sending me to Kangaamiut was the right thing to do, regardless of the result. The police did not have infinite resources. They were already stretched thinly across Greenland's vast and challenging geography, but it didn't take much to bring hope to those who had none.

It might be a small gesture, but it was something. It was a start.

"If we don't find Iiva," Tuukula said. "Then we will help her mother to grieve, so that Iiva will live on in her memory."

"And Iiva's father? What about him?"

I thought about Saamoq taking his rifle into the mountains. He wouldn't be the first Greenlander, overcome by grief, to choose a more drastic way to ease his pain. I worried that our search for Iiva might end with more than one missing person.

"I don't know," Tuukula said. "I will know more when we visit the house."

We didn't have to wait long. Luui stopped on the road next to a short rocky path leading to the door of a wooden house painted blue. The paint was fresh and had yet to be ravaged by summer winds loaded with sand, or the winter winds with sharp frosty breath. Luui scuffed her feet in the grit on the road as Kilaala said goodbye to the women who had followed her home. It seemed that we had replaced them, that now it was up to us to help Kilaala through the next stage of the search for her daughter. I took Luui's hand at the start of the path and followed her into Kilaala's home.

Kilaala chattered as we removed our shoes. I dumped my daypack on top of Tuukula's holdall and followed Luui into the lounge. The walls, like many homes in Greenland were plastered with photographs, most of them framed, some tucked into the corners of bigger frames, or tacked to the wall. The outer wall of Kilaala's lounge reminded me of a detective's notice board, the kind I'd seen in the movies or on television. There must have been over fifty photographs on the wall, and I took a moment to study them, as Kilaala made tea and coffee, with the promise of something sweeter for Luui.

Most of the photographs were of Iiva, and I recognised the one they had used on the national news when reporting the developments of the search. Iiva and Luui shared some similarities, not least their round cheeks. But Iiva's lip captured my attention, and a series of photos showed the progression from an angry red groove and stitches, to a softer white scar that divided her top lip. Iiva smiled in almost every photograph, even those taken shortly after her operation, when she was smaller than Luui.

I turned as Kilaala rattled a tray of mugs and a plate of raisin bread into the living room, sliding it onto the table before she joined me at the wall of photographs. Kilaala pointed at each one in turn, talking me through Iiva's childhood with a little help from Tuukula.

"Always happy," he said, nodding as Kilaala added more detail here, pointing at another photograph there. "Always smiling, even when she couldn't."

"Her eyes," Kilaala said, in Danish, and I knew exactly what she meant.

Iiva's eyes shone in almost every single photograph, even those that were wrinkled and torn – saved, perhaps, from enthusiastic and loving fingers.

"And this one?" I asked, pointing at the only photograph in which Iiva looked sad.

She was holding something dark in her hands,

pressed against the wrinkles of her stripey t-shirt. The contrast made it difficult to see, and I waited for Tuukula to translate Kilaala's words. He nodded as she spoke, and again when she finished.

"That was the day Iiva found the dead ravens," he said. "The adults had died, leaving the orphans she found in the nest."

"I know about them," I said, as I recalled what Ulaajuk told me back in the cell in Nuuk.

"There is more to tell," Tuukula said, as Kilaala gestured for us to join her at the table.

11

Tuukula took a sip of coffee before settling into the role of translator. Kilaala sat down on the side of the table opposite the window, giving me the impression that she wanted to be able to see outside, to see the road and the people passing the house, just in case one of them was Iiva. I pushed back my chair as Luui clambered into my lap. She really was heavier than I remembered, and I caught Kilaala's eye as Luui made herself comfortable. Kilaala gave me a knowing look, together with a smile that I imagined might be shared between mothers all over Greenland. Tuukula shook his head, ever so slightly, but enough to catch my attention, suggesting that this was not the time to ruin the illusion. So, for the remainder of our time in Kangaamiut, or at least the time we spent at the table, Luui was my daughter. I fussed with Luui's hair as Kilaala started to talk, pausing every now and again for Tuukula to translate.

"It was the winter she turned five," Tuukula said, as Kilaala dipped a cube of sugar into her coffee and sucked at it. "Iiva found a raven's nest on a path running above the last line of houses." Tuukula added something in Greenlandic, and Kilaala nodded as he pointed to the north and east. "She was with her mother," he said. "And Kilaala helped her carry the two raven chicks home."

"Saamoq doesn't like ravens," Kilaala said in Danish.

I could only imagine why.

Ravens are the ubiquitous bird of the north, staying year-round, through the long summers and dark winters. They are hardy and wily, and I remembered seeing ravens on the streetlights one autumn, when it was still too light to trigger the bulbs, but cold enough for snow and freezing temperatures. More than once, I thought I saw the big black birds covering the lamps with their wings to fool the lights into thinking it was darker than it was, turning on the lights and drawing heat from the bulbs.

Hardy and wily.

"And noisy," Tuukula said, as Kilaala continued her story. "Iiva hid the orphan ravens in the shed, feeding them fish from Saamoq's drying racks, and flakes of dry whale meat."

Tuukula smiled at the thought, and I pictured his drying racks on the beach in Qaanaaq, the very north of Greenland. That thought led to another, and suddenly I was on the sledge heading north, until Luui tapped my thigh and I realised that, still tired, my mind had wandered. I tuned into Kilaala's story at the moment her husband discovered the ravens.

"Saamoq was angry," Tuukula said. "The ravens had shit everywhere and had plucked the stitches from his sealskins." He laughed, and I imagined that the thought of ravens getting inside a hunter's shed was unthinkable. "Saamoq found Iiva on the floor of the shed talking to the ravens."

"How?" I asked, remembering to look at Kilaala.

Tuukula waited for Kilaala to speak before answering for her. "She mimicked the noises they made, the cawing, the shrieking and that..." He paused, searching for the words in Danish.

"The water drop," I said, frowning for lack of a better way to describe it. Everybody knew what it was, we had all heard it. But even as children we struggled to emulate it. It was as if the raven could drop the note from its throat to its toes, echoing dully on the way down.

"*Aap*," Tuukula said. "Iiva spent all her time in the shed for a week, and then, after Saamoq turfed the ravens into the snow, she would sit on the deck, with the ravens on the railings. Iiva fed them and they talked to her. She made the same noises that she'd learned from the ravens."

"And that was the first time she spoke," Kilaala said.

"What?"

"Iiva had an operation to seal the hole in her palate and to close her lip before she was eight months old," Tuukula said, pausing as Kilaala explained. "When she was older she could only make sounds. She struggled to say whole words, as if she couldn't get her tongue around them."

I was tempted to pull out my notebook, to recall what I had read of the hole in the palate of a child with a cleft palate, and how the air – and food – would escape up the child's nose. Eating and speaking were difficult. They were skills that had to be learned and practised. If Iiva had been in

Maniitsoq, she might have had a speech therapist. She would definitely have had one in Nuuk. But in Kangaamiut? I wondered.

Both Tuukula and Kilaala were quiet, waiting for me to return from my thoughts.

"Sorry," I said. "I was wondering if Iiva had a speech therapist. Someone to help her."

Kilaala spoke and Tuukula nodded, creasing his lips in a knowing smile.

"She had the ravens," he said.

"*Saamoq*," Kilaala said, pausing as she framed her words in Greenlandic, before trying them again in her halting Danish. "He said she had a raven tongue."

Tuukula smiled again, glancing at Luui, raising his eyebrows at the thought of Iiva talking with ravens when she was just five years old.

"*Naamik*," Kilaala said. "It was not good."

"Why?" I asked.

I had to wait as Kilaala struggled through a long explanation, one which flattened Tuukula's smile, and revealed a deeper pain that Kilaala carried. It seemed the thing that helped her daughter the most, was the very thing to drive Iiva and her father apart.

"He hates ravens," Kilaala said.

"Why?"

"Scavengers and thieves," Tuukula said. "That's what he called them." He paused again when Kilaala spoke, before adding, "He didn't want his daughter to learn the language of thieves, and he shooed them away."

Luui turned in my lap as Kilaala left the table to pluck a photograph from the wall. She returned to the table, pausing by my side to slide the photograph in front of me. She brushed a tear from her cheek, but not before one fell onto the photograph, glistening in the spring light shining through the window.

"He killed one of them," Tuukula said, repeating it in Greenlandic.

Kilaala sniffed once as she nodded, and then sat down.

Luui shifted in my lap to get a closer look at the photograph. She gently wiped Kilaala's tears from Iiva's cheeks with her tiny thumbs, and then cawed, just once, as ravens do.

The raven tongue was the language of thieves, according to Iiva's father. It made me wonder if Iiva had indeed gone missing, lost in the mountains, or if she had been stolen.

"And then," Tuukula said, as he translated. "Just a few days ago, Iiva found another nest."

12

Ravens are survivors. And, with Iiva's help, according to Kilaala, Iiva had been determined to help the new raven young to survive, even if it meant hiding them from her father.

There were ravens in the mountains around Qinngorput, the area where I lived in Nuuk. They flew down the steep walls of black granite, the same walls that revealed winter's progress as it crept down the mountain to the east of the apartment blocks, the store, and the school. But unlike Nuuk, the houses of Kangaamiut were built on the mountainside, staggered from the sea, as if one day, far into the future, they might stretch all the way to the summit.

Thinking about survival and thinking about life in a remote Arctic village, perched on the cliffs, just a stone's throw from the black Greenland seas, I wondered just how different the Greenlanders were from the ravens. Neither human nor bird flew south for the winter. They weathered the same storms as the Greenlanders did, sheltering between the same rocks, at the mercy of the weather systems curling around the same mountain peaks. Surely Saamoq should have understood, perhaps even embraced his daughter's connection with the ravens.

"You don't understand," Tuukula said, as he sat

on a rock on the path, smoking his roll-up cigarette until the burning tobacco flaked at his fingertip.

"What don't I understand?"

"The effort it takes to catch the fish, to land the whale. How hard it is for Saamoq to provide for his family."

I had heard it before, but this time, with Kilaala's tears and the much loved and wrinkled photograph of her daughter fresh in my memory, I wasn't interested in defending Saamoq Suersaq.

Not in the slightest.

"He took away the one thing that was helping his daughter."

"The ravens followed her to school, Petra. Think on that," Tuukula said.

"One of them did," I said. "He killed the other one – one of the first ones. Remember?"

"*Aap.*" Tuukula finished his cigarette. He plucked another from behind his ear, shrugging when I stared at him. "I'm travelling," he said. "I'm allowed two cigarettes a day."

"I don't care how much you smoke," I said. "I'm worried about Iiva."

"And her *ataata*," Tuukula said. "You should worry about him too."

I *was* worried about him. I looked up and along the path, wrinkling my nose in the thin cloud of smoke from Tuukula's cigarette, as I pictured Saamoq wandering the mountains, searching for his daughter, or perhaps searching for a place to die.

"Then think of Saamoq and his daughter," Tuukula continued. "He is powerless to help her. At least, from his own way of thinking." Tuukula paused to look up the path to where Luui was channelling a stream of meltwater with lichen-covered rocks and handfuls of pebbles. "He understands he must provide for his daughter. It's the only thing he can do – putting meat on their table, selling the rest. But he can't talk to her – at least he feels that she cannot talk to him. He leaves her alone, for that reason. Meanwhile, he struggles to repair his hunting gear. He must keep a store of food for his dogs, covering the racks with nets to dry the fish in the wind ready for the summer. The nets keep the ravens away from the fish, but then he worries about the flies, when they arrive in the spring. So, he dries too much fish too soon, and the racks are heavy. The ravens are smart," Tuukula said, tapping his head with the stub of his shortened finger, the one he lost in a hunting accident. "They use their weight to tip a spar of wood. So Saamoq chases them away, hammering another spar with more nails." Tuukula took another drag on his cigarette, watching me as he puffed the smoke in a small cloud above his head. "And it goes on, every day." He paused at my questioning look. "You believe in the ravens? That they helped Iiva to speak?"

"If she tried to copy them, yes," I said. "Maybe."

"You think they helped train her muscles?"

"Like a speech therapist would teach her to do."

"Different sounds, needing different muscles. Lots of practice."

"And then Saamoq put an end to that."

"Because," Tuukula said, "his feelings towards

ravens are different to hers."

"And he couldn't see it."

"We don't know what he saw or what he sees. To know that we have to find him."

"You mean we have to look for Saamoq before we can look for Iiva?"

Tuukula finished his second cigarette. "*Imaqa*. But what's that over there," he said, with a nod towards Luui waving from the top of a boulder further along the path. "Maybe she has found something."

I walked beside Tuukula in silence, wondering if I had said too much. It was all so frustrating. We needed a practical piece of evidence, something that could lead us to the next step, and the one after that, until the missing person was found. At least, those were my thoughts as I walked beside Tuukula on the path leading up and into the mountains of Kangaamiut. It was the shaman's daughter who found the first practical lead in the search for Iiva.

"Shoes?" I said, as I crouched beside a small pair of shoes on the path. They were too big for Luui – she had already tried them on – and too small for an adult or a teenager.

"They must be Iiva's," Tuukula said.

"You think so?"

"The original search team found another pair further up the mountain," he said. "You told me that."

"Yes, but wouldn't they have found this pair first, on the way up the path?"

"They should have, unless…"

I caught the quizzical look on Tuukula's face,

and, in a sudden burst of light as the clouds evaporated in the sun, I saw my own reflection in his eyes – just as quizzical, equally curious.

"Unless," I said, "they were left here recently." I felt my brow wrinkle, just above my nose, the way Atii said it did when I was puzzling things out. "But then they could be anybody's."

Luui said something to her father, then clambered down the other side of the rock, leaping the last metre to land in a patch of refrozen snow, like a dune of hailstones. She called for us to come. As we rounded the boulder she lifted up a stripey t-shirt, pressing it against her chest as if trying it on. Unlike the shoes, the t-shirt was the right size, and I remembered another five-year-old girl who had one just like it.

"Iiva's," I said. "From the photograph."

"When she was five years old." Tuukula looked up, scanning the lower outcrops of rock rising up the steep sides of the mountain.

We found more of Iiva's old clothes just off the path – a pair of cotton trousers, and a thin summer hat, hanging from a cross of wood clinched between a small cairn of Greenland rocks.

"A scarecrow?" I said. "Like in a farmer's field."

"There are no crows in Greenland," Tuukula said, as he studied the wooden cross. He pressed a cracked thumbnail into the wood, then sniffed at the oil that seeped onto it. "Fish," he said. "And seal."

"Someone built a figure of stones and wood, and dressed it with Iiva's clothes," I said, as my frown deepened to a pinch. "To scare the ravens away?"

"Maybe not to scare them away," Tuukula said. "Maybe to attract them."

"That doesn't make any sense," I said.

"Not to us," Tuukula said.

He looked down and smiled as Luui took his hand. She flapped her free arm like a wing, and then cawed like a raven, the same sound over and over, in the way that Greenlandic children did, all over the country. Except, in Kangaamiut, there was one girl who knew all the sounds, the whole raven vocabulary.

"We should follow the path," I said.

"*Naamik*," Tuukula said. "They've already tried that. We should follow the clothes."

13

Luui led the way, scrambling off the path before slipping over slick black rocks, bald of snow, melted in the sun. I gathered up Iiva's clothes, and then followed Tuukula as he beat a trail between the rocks, picking his way up the mountain after Luui. I wondered when her little legs would start to tire, and when I might get a break. But Luui possessed a hidden energy that seemed to lift her from one bald rock to the next. Tuukula called for her to slow down, but Luui just waved, jabbing her tiny fingers at the ravens scrabbling about the rocks above.

"She's ignoring me," Tuukula said during a brief pause. We both watched as Luui continued to climb. "We'll have to talk later."

Since meeting Tuukula and his young daughter, I had often wondered about his approach to parenting. Like the children of many Greenlandic families, Luui seemed to enjoy a lot of freedom, with few noticeable boundaries. The boundaries of my own childhood had been drawn by child psychologists and pedagogues, enforced by strict curfews and regular evaluations. I used to envy the other children at school, how they could stay out late, even in winter, when I was scolded for the slightest infractions. As for Luui, now high up on the mountainside, it seemed her only limit was the sky itself, and gravity, keeping her feet on the ground, not including her short leaps between the boulders.

A raven's cry caught my attention, and I scanned the sky – bright now that the sun had burned fully through the cloud. There were at least four ravens – two on the wing, one cawing and clacking along a ridge halfway up a sheer rock wall, and the fourth hopping closer and closer to Luui.

"*Ataata*," Luui shouted. And then, in Danish, "Hurry."

Luui pointed at the raven and we picked up the pace, slipping and sliding up steep banks of melted snow, pressing our palms on stubby black lichen when we fell. Luui called again, urging us onwards and upwards with shrill calls, not unlike those of the raven.

"I need a break," I said, as I dropped Iiva's shoes. I knelt on the snow, gathered Iiva's shoes into my arms, and then tried to stuff them into my jacket pockets. Tuukula called out for Luui to stop, swearing when she didn't.

"These past few years have been challenging," he said, as he sat on a rock beside me.

"The past *few* years?"

"*Aap*. All of them. And every year she's stronger, more curious."

"She's only five," I said.

"And I am seventy-one." Tuukula laughed. "She's my first and only child. Never again. No more."

"I must admit," I said. "I'm impressed you've come this far."

"Up the mountain?"

"With Luui. Without help, I mean."

Tuukula shrugged, and said, "I wouldn't be able to keep up, if I didn't use a little magic in between. Only, this last year…"

I looked at Tuukula as his words tapered into thoughts. "Magic?"

"Just a little," he said with a shrug. "I ask the spirits to make her drowsy when I'm tired. Most of the time they listen, and oblige, but lately…" Tuukula paused to laugh, and I caught a flash of what looked like admiration in his eyes. "Lately, when I talk to the spirits, Luui seems to make them a better offer. I should be pleased, and I am, but I'm also tired, Petra. My daughter wears me out."

"She wears both of us out," I said, as I succeeded in zipping half of each shoe into my pockets. I pushed myself onto my feet and reached out for Tuukula's hand. "Come on," I said. "We'd better catch her up."

Tuukula took my hand, and I smiled at the warm dry touch of his wrinkled skin. We took it in turns to lead, pulling each other across slippery patches of snow, hauling each other over boulders. The ravens cawed above us, and, when we reached a flat area big enough for a house, Luui welcomed us with a cry of her own.

"Hurry," she said, pointing at a large crack in the rock, slicing a deep granite gash into the mountain.

"Wait," Tuukula said, as Luui slipped onto her belly to squirm through the crack.

Tuukula ran forwards, finding his second wind

as his daughter poked her head and shoulders inside the mountain. I ran alongside him, skidding onto my knees and reaching for Luui's feet as she turned to one side, determined to crawl all the way into the crack. I held the heel of her shoe for a moment before she tugged it free of my grasp.

"Luui," Tuukula said, as he lay on the rocks to shout into the mountain. "You must come back." He spoke in Danish, and I wondered if he switched between languages depending upon the impression he was trying to make on Luui. The greatest impression of her disappearance, however, could be seen on Tuukula's face, as he slapped his palm on the rock.

"We'll never get in there," I said. "She'll have to come back herself."

Tuukula pressed his face into the crack. "It's too steep," he said. "If she goes any further in, she won't be able to crawl back by herself. She'll need a rope. *We* need a rope."

"And help," I said. "One of us has to go back."

Everything changed in that moment, when the search for one girl turned into a rescue for another. *And I brought her here,* I thought, as I wondered what might have made Luui clamber up the mountain and then dive through a hole in the rock. I heard the clack of raven claws on the rocks above me and looked up to stare into the beady black eye of a male. A moment passed, and I could feel a shallow wave of empathy for Iiva's father. I wanted to blame the raven for encouraging Luui to crawl into danger. But it was just a raven. At least, that's what I told myself, as I checked my smartphone, cursing at the lack of signal.

"You stay here," I said to Tuukula. "I'll get help."

"And a rope," he said, calling after me, as I started back down the mountain, slipping and sliding towards the path below.

14

Running down the mountain was harder than climbing up it. I lost track of how many times I slipped, thudding the base of my palms into rocks, feeling the dull creep of pain that increased each time I broke my fall.

But I was making progress.

I covered the same distance we had climbed in half the time, including the time I spent on my butt. When I reached the path, I had to pause to check my surroundings. I found the wooden cross and turned away from it, running down the path towards the village. My hair clung to my forehead in strands and I brushed them away, tucking them behind my ear or just letting them fly behind me as I increased speed. I was hot in my jacket but loathe to slow down to remove it. Keeping a steady rhythm was the key, anticipating the dips and grooves in the path, leaping onto one smooth-topped boulder and then scanning, hoping – sometimes attaching a silent prayer – that there would be another boulder to leap onto. But each time I mouthed the prayer I was already airborne, flying along the path with Iiva's shoes half-zipped into my pockets and her stripey t-shirt tucked into my utility belt.

I approached a long bend in the path, giddy at the sight of the roofs of the first houses below. I picked up speed, jogging a list of priorities through my mind. There had to be a volunteer fire department. They would have the equipment needed to rescue Luui. Perhaps it was still attached to the quad bikes – if they had quad bikes – from when they were searching for Iiva Suersaq. A doctor would be ideal, but the village, like so many other villages and settlements in Greenland, would likely only have an untrained medical assistant, traditionally known as the village midwife. My own medical training would have to suffice, and I wondered just what I could expect, what injuries Luui might have sustained deep inside the mountain.

As I ran down the steep path I had no idea how far Luui might have gone into the mountain, or how hurt she might be. Nor did it matter, as I careened at full speed into a man walking up it.

The man fell into the old snow and tough Arctic grasses just off the path. I slid over his body, turning a complete cartwheel before shuddering to a full stop. Everything hurt more than I wanted to think about. I almost laughed at the jumble of my thoughts, the mix of pain and potential chastisement as I rolled onto my side to apologise to the man. But when I saw the rifle levelled at my chest and heard the click and clack of the bolt as the man jacked a bullet into the chamber, I wondered just how much I had hurt him.

"I'm so sorry," I said in Danish. "I didn't see you."

The man, about the same height as me, and taller than Tuukula, kept his gaze fixed on my middle, and I looked down to see Iiva's shoes poking out of my jacket pockets, and her t-shirt flapping in a gust of wind twisting dirt along the path.

"Those don't belong to you," the man said. "Where did you get them?"

"These shoes?" I tried to catch the man's eye but failed. "I believe they belong to Iiva Suersaq. She's the girl who went missing just a few days ago."

Of course, I guessed that he must know that, and not just because the whole village had been on the alert to find Iiva, but because this man was her father.

"You're Saamoq Suersaq," I said, taking a step forward. "Aren't you?"

"Don't come any closer," he said, waving the end of the rifle in my direction. He lifted his head, briefly, but just long enough to make eye contact.

"I'm a police officer," I said. "I'm looking for Iiva."

"You have her clothes."

"Yes. I found them on the path." I pointed up the mountain, curious to see if the man would look the same way. When he didn't, I wondered what he knew about the effigy on the path. "I found them by a wooden cross, stuck between a pile of rocks. Do you know about that? Saamoq?"

The man reacted when I said his name, flashing me a hard stare as he raised the rifle, tugging the stock into his shoulder as if he was about to fire.

"Saamoq," I said. "Listen, I'm a police officer. I'm here to help."

"You have Iiva's clothes."

"Yes," I said, teasing my fingers around Iiva's t-shirt. "Yes, I do."

"You should have left them where you found them. They are not meant for you."

"Are they for Iiva?" I asked, wondering if he knew where she was, or if he expected her to come to the path for her clothes, even her old ones. Then he pulled the trigger. The bullet slammed into the crusty snow just an arm's length to my right, and I decided any further questions could wait. I glanced over my shoulder and leaped further from the path to slide down a tongue of old snow and gritty ice, fumbling to pull my pistol from its holster, as Saamoq ran after me.

15

My pistol slipped out of my hand as I slammed my ribs into an exposed head of granite. The impact knocked the air out of my lungs and I fought for breath as Saamoq slid down the snow towards me, into a sitting position with his hands around his rifle, the barrel pointed at my chest. I saw my pistol in a hollow of snow just below me, and I reached for it, only to pull back my hand as Saamoq fired for a second time. The shot echoed around the mountain walls until the old snow absorbed it.

"For God's sake, Saamoq," I yelled, as my initial fear twisted into frustration. "I'm a police officer. Put your gun down."

Maybe I was more pissed than frustrated, losing my grip on my professionalism as I slipped and scrabbled to my feet, brushing snow out of the creases around my trouser pockets, and fixing Saamoq with an angry look as he slid to a stop in front of me.

Planned or not, it seemed to work.

Saamoq lowered his rifle, before slinging it over his shoulder as he stood up.

"I know you're upset, Saamoq. I know you're looking for your daughter…"

I was ready to say more, but the words died on my lips as Saamoq dipped his chin to his chest and covered his eyes with his hands. He shook as he sobbed, silently, the tears welling beneath his palms, before dribbling in slow streams along his thumbs.

"It's my fault," he said, as he lifted his head. Saamoq wiped the tears from his cheeks, sniffing several times as he caught his breath. "But she brought more birds home. *Tulugaq* – ravens."

"I know," I said.

"I knew she would go into the mountains. I know she has a hiding place somewhere up here." Saamoq looked around, staring at the walls of granite. "I just don't know where."

"And you didn't tell anybody? What about the people searching for her?" I thought about the Challenger jet, and how, if Iiva was hidden underground, if she was deep enough, even the thermal cameras wouldn't find her.

"What would I tell them? That I scared my daughter into the mountains?"

"Yes," I said. "Exactly that."

"And then what?" Saamoq's lip curled as his face twisted beneath heavy black brows. "What would they think? Would they think I had done something to her? That I might have hurt her? *Naamik*," he said, shaking his head. "I would never hurt her, but those ravens…"

I tensed as Saamoq's hand drifted towards his rifle.

"Tell me about Iiva," I said, pitching my voice between us, softer than the wind teasing our clothes, but loud enough, I hoped, to show him I was listening, that I wanted to hear his side of the story.

I spared a thought for Luui and Tuukula but resisted the urge to run to the village – any sudden movement might send Saamoq over the edge, an edge that he was barely clinging to.

"I'm not a bad man," he said. "But I'm not a good father." Saamoq lifted his head, drawing strength from his words. A confession of sorts. "Kilaala loved Iiva from before she was born. And I thought I did too. But then, when there were problems, and the doctors said Iiva would need surgery, that she would need help to breathe and to eat, and that later, she would need help to talk. It was too much. Life is hard enough without such things. I have seen it. Weakness is death. My daughter was born weak – weaker than normal. I thought she would die as a baby, and I prepared myself. I let her go when I should have loved her. But if I loved her, and she died, what then? What would I do? I had to be strong for Kilaala. She would be crushed when Iiva died. I believed it was only a matter of time."

Saamoq looked into my eyes, and I held his gaze, nodding ever so slightly, encouraging him to continue. As alien as it seemed, I could almost understand his reaction, how he prepared himself to cope with what he thought was inevitable. As heartless as it was, it almost made sense as a coping mechanism – survival at its most primal.

"She didn't die," Saamoq looked away, staring up at the mountains. "But I had already distanced myself. I was convinced she would still die, if not one day, then the next. And when she didn't the gap between us was too great. I saw her weakness as my weakness. Her scar on her lip reminded me every day. So I stopped looking. Her voice – those breathy words – reminded me how weak I was every time I heard her speak, so I stopped listening. It was my way – the only way. Until the ravens."

Saamoq turned back to me, and I almost started at the fire in his eyes.

"The ravens, those thieves, they stole my daughter from me. When she found that first nest – she was just five years old. She brought those ravens home. Then I couldn't ignore her. I couldn't ignore the screeching from the shed. So loud. Every time I heard those birds, I would shout and curse. I made my wife cry. I made her run away to the bedroom. But my daughter was already gone, hiding in the shed. Then, when the screeching got louder and louder, I went to the shed. There was so much screeching, I thought there were more ravens, not just two tiny birds. When I opened the shed, I saw Iiva with these birds in her hands, wearing that t-shirt." Saamoq sneered as he pointed at my belt. "Iiva was screeching like the ravens, louder and louder. I shouted at her to stop. I think it was the first time I ever talked *to* my daughter," Saamoq said, before clasping his hand to his mouth. He let his hand fall, drawing a thin stream of saliva with it as more tears welled in his eyes. "My first words to Iiva, the first time I ever really said anything to her, were curses and shouts. I was angry. It's no wonder she ran away."

"She's run away before?"

"*Aap*," he said. "She grabbed those birds when I tried to take them. And she ran away. She was gone the rest of the day. When she came back, when her mother finally got her into bed, plucking those damned birds from her arms, I took them." Saamoq shook his head slowly as he wrung his hands around imaginary necks. "I killed the first one, and I dropped its body into the snow outside the shed. I left it there as I hunted for the second one. I forgot about the dead one. And I never found its brother. I should have thrown the body away. When Iiva found it, I remember thinking I was pleased she saw it. And then her mother took that photo."

"I've seen it," I said, softly.

"Over the years, so many times, I've tried to rip that photo in two. But each time I put it back," he said, lifting his hand in front of him, as if tucking the photograph back into the corner of the frame, exactly as I had found it.

"And then Iiva found more ravens," I said. "Is that what happened?"

"Just the other day," Saamoq said, and nodded. "Another abandoned nest. She brought them home, and when I saw them, I got mad. I chased her out of the house, and she ran away. She was gone for more than a day, and Kilaala called the police." He paused to look at me, as if seeing my uniform for the first time. "I knew she would come back. But when they stopped searching, and Kilaala got so upset, I knew I had to find her."

"So you went into the mountains."

"*Aap*," he said, pointing at Iiva's shoes in my pockets and her t-shirt tucked into my belt. "I knew she wouldn't come if I called, so I decided to bring her to me." He shook his head, suppressing a laugh as if the thought of what he did embarrassed him. "People say I'm crazy, and maybe they're right. But I know ravens," he said, jabbing his finger in the air between us. Then he tapped his forehead, and said, "I know how they think. They're curious. They are drawn to my daughter – she calls to them with her raven tongue. They know her clothes, her smell. So I made an Iiva. I made my daughter – stone dolls with her clothes, her smell, in different places in the mountains. You found one. I made more. Then when the ravens came, I shot at them, killing some before they got smart and left the dolls alone. Then I realised how stupid I had been. I thought if the ravens came, then so would Iiva. And now that I have taught the ravens to fear my daughter, they will never come to her, and I will never find her. She is gone."

16

The snow crunched and squeaked as Saamoq sank to his knees in front of me. His rifle slipped from his shoulder and I took it, slinging it across my chest before reaching down into the hollow for my pistol. I watched Saamoq struggle in the wake of his confession as I holstered my pistol and snapped the cover closed. I pulled my smartphone from my pocket and sighed at the sight of three bars of signal. Constable Jiihu Eliassen answered my call from the station in Maniitsoq after just two rings, promising to contact the local volunteer fire chief as soon as I hung up.

"We have to go, Saamoq," I said, slipping my phone back into my pocket.

"Where?"

"There's a little girl who needs our help."

"Iiva?"

I shook my head. "My friend and his daughter."

Saamoq's story had given me some hope that maybe Iiva wasn't that far away after all. "If you help me help my friends, then I promise I won't leave Kangaamiut until we have found Iiva."

We picked our way across the snow to the path to begin our climb back up the mountain. I heard the chatter of small engines and smiled as I realised the volunteer fire department did have quad bikes.

Saamoq and I stepped to one side of the path as they approached.

"Up there," I said. "There's a crack in a rock."

"We know it," the fire chief said.

"You'll have to go on foot," I said.

"Not if we follow the path. It curves around the top and comes back down to that boulder."

"Boulder? I thought it was part of the mountain."

"*Aap*," he said. "It sheared off the mountain a long time ago. It's a boulder now."

I saw the frown on the fire chief's face, as if he was wondering why they hadn't looked there earlier, during the search for Iiva.

"It's okay," I said. "You were never going to find Iiva. Not if she didn't want to be found."

"Who crawled beneath the boulder?"

"Her name is Luui." I fought back a smile as I said her name. "And I have a feeling she is about to surprise us all."

The feeling grew stronger with every step we took along the path.

The three men from the volunteer fire department raced up the path, ploughing into the snow to curve around the larger boulders where possible. By the time we arrived at the boulder, they were rigging ropes and anchors in anticipation of crawling into the crack in the rock.

"They're too big," Tuukula said, as Saamoq and I approached. "I offered to go, but they told me I'm too old." He paused to look at Saamoq, nodding once before turning back to me. "I said you would go."

"Me?"

"You're taller than me, but slimmer than anyone here."

At any other time, it might have been a complement, but the practical aspect of rescuing Luui, kept me focused, and without another word I started to unbuckle my utility belt.

"Wait."

I looked up as the fire chief held up his hand, clicking his fingers to get our attention.

"What is it?"

"We heard something."

"Luui?" Tuukula asked.

"That's your little girl?" The fire chief nodded "*Aap*, it could have been her. Come," he said, beckoning Tuukula closer to the crack in the rock. I knelt beside the shaman as he pressed his face beneath the boulder, as far as he could.

"Luui?"

"*Ataata*," Luui shouted back, bringing a smile to all our faces.

Tuukula said something in Greenlandic, before translating for me. "I said we have a rope." He paused, as Luui replied. "But she says she doesn't need it. She says there's a way out."

Tuukula pulled his head out of the crack and stood up. He pointed to the left, then jogged along the side of the boulder. I fastened my belt and followed, with Saamoq and the fire crew right behind me.

We heard the two girls a moment before we saw them, catching a flash of black feathers as Iiva released a young raven from her hands into the wind. I caught my breath, trying to stem a sudden rush of emotion as I looked at her. I failed, and the tears trickled down my cheeks as the two girls walked towards us, hand in hand, taking it in turns to call to the ravens above them.

"Iiva," Saamoq said, sinking to his knees as she stopped, hesitating, until Luui gripped her hand and tugged her around the last few rocks and into her father's arms.

"Magic," Luui said, pointing at Iiva wrapped in her father's embrace.

"*Aap*," Tuukula said. He knelt down to brush at the dirt on Luui's cheeks, licking his thumbs to rub at the stubborn patches, revealing her freckles and releasing a bout of giggles that reverberated around the rocks.

I stepped around the shaman and his daughter for a better look at Iiva. It was her eyes that caught me, as they burned with a new energy, hope, perhaps, for the future. She was taller than Luui, older by six years, but both girls possessed the strength and will power to make the impossible happen.

"Thank you," Iiva said, in Danish, with an almost imperceptible nasal inflection.

"You're very welcome," I said.

The fire chief tapped me on the shoulder, before nodding at Iiva and Saamoq. "We'll help them down the mountain, then come back for you."

"It's okay," I said. "I'd like to walk."

Tuukula nodded that he and Luui would do the same. We waited for Iiva and her father to climb onto the quad bikes. Luui waved as they pulled away.

"Now, Luui," Tuukula said, as he pulled his daughter into his arms. "We have to have a little talk."

Luui pressed her fingers to his lips, pinching them shut as she shook her head.

"Magic," I said, as I led the way back to the path.

17

The fire chief had arranged mattresses and bedding on the first floor of the garage housing the gear and quad bikes. Luui swapped her raven shrieks for the shriek of a motorbike as she steered one of the stationary quads on an imaginary journey. Tuukula smoked outside, while I clambered up the stairs and flopped onto the nearest mattress.

I don't remember waking to eat, although Tuukula assured me that I did.

I vaguely remember lots of chattering, and the bounce of small bodies from one mattress to the next, but anything else is nothing more than a sleepy blur.

"You had a long talk with Kilaala," Tuukula said, as we sat at a table inside the boat on the way back to Maniitsoq.

"I did?"

"*Aap*," he said. "She told everybody what you said, that you would find her daughter. And you did."

"Luui did," I said.

"She played her part. We all did."

Tuukula fiddled with a tin of tobacco, rolling two cigarettes on the table. He stuck one behind his ear and pinched the other between his lips.

"Two, when travelling," I said.

Tuukula smiled, and then excused himself to go for a smoke on the deck. I heard the patter of Luui's small feet as she left the children's play area to join her father outside. The wind tugged at her hair and curled the smoke from Tuukula's cigarette over the railings. I felt a lump in my throat as I watched father and daughter teasing each other on the deck. There might be sixty-six years between them, but I struggled to think of another father and daughter that could be closer. I wondered about my own father, but having never met him, I struggled to recall his face. I shrugged and reached for my coffee, sipping at it as we sailed south to Maniitsoq.

I left Tuukula and Luui at the airport in Maniitsoq, peeling Luui's hands from my neck before kissing her cheek and promising that we would see each other again.

"Soon," Tuukula said.

"I hope so," I said.

My flight landed first, and I joined the other passengers as they boarded the plane, then turned to wave as Luui squeezed past the Air Greenland service staff to shout one last goodbye.

I slept on the plane, waking first as the wheels bumped down on the runway in Nuuk, and then again when the stewardess gently rubbed my shoulder.

"You're home," she said.

"Yes."

I was the last to leave the plane, leaning into the wind at door of the Dash 7, before climbing down the steps to walk to the airport building. I smiled as

I spotted the same police officer I had seen on leaving Nuuk, drawing closer as the lines of passengers arriving and departing merged in the tiny Arctic airport.

"I'm Petra," I said, pressing my hand into his. "We saw each other a few days ago."

"*Iiji*," he said.

"And your name?"

"Maratse," he said, with a brief dip of his head.

The End

Acknowledgements

As with many of my novels and novellas, I would be lost without the support and editing skills of Isabel Muir. Isabel writes cosy mysteries under her pen name *Isabella Muir*.

Special mention for help in writing *The Girl with the Raven Tongue* goes to my mother. As a trained speech and language therapist, my mum provided lots of answers to my *what if?* questions. However, the accuracy of the information about cleft lips and cleft palates, and the plausibility of a young girl training herself to speak by mimicking ravens, rests on my shoulders alone, as it was me who chose to incorporate a few facts here, while adding heaps of dramatic licence there.

As with so many of my Greenland stories, they are deeply personal in the sense that I learned so much from the Greenlandic people, and the environment of Greenland, during the seven years I lived there. *The Girl with the Raven Tongue*, however, takes on an added personal dimension, when I say that I was born with a *bifid uvula* (also known as a cleft uvula). It's the thing that hangs down in the back of your throat. Mine is split, or forked. According to my mother, I was just a hair's breadth away from having a cleft lip and cleft palate. Apart from being a constant source of amusement and interest for my mother's speech therapist friends, as a child I often experienced problems eating, with food going up my nose instead of down my throat. Swallowing tablets is still problematic. As is laughing when eating – but when isn't it?

While I can't pretend to have experienced the challenges of growing up with a cleft lip or cleft palate, it did make the story more interesting to write.

Lastly, I am very excited about the next novella in the Greenland Missing Persons series: *The Shiver in the Arctic*.

Chris
July 2020
Denmark

CONSTABLE PETRA JENSEN 1-3

The Shiver in the Arctic

Greenland Missing Persons #3

CHRISTOFFER PETERSEN

Author's Note

The Shiver in the Arctic is the third novella in the Greenland Missing Persons series featuring Constable Petra Piitalaat Jensen. Readers of my other novellas will know that I like to experiment a little with each story, whereas the novels are more uniform in style. So, if this novella tastes a little like a *whodunnit*, then you're not wrong, your eyes are not deceiving you, although I sincerely hope you will be deceived at some point in the story.

The Shiver in the Arctic is packed with cultural Easter eggs, bringing a little slice of Greenland into your life. It is also longer than my usual novellas and for that I blame Petra.

Chris
July 2020
Denmark

CONSTABLE PETRA JENSEN 1-3

1

It was the magazine article that did it. From the moment Sergeant Kiiu "George" Duneq discovered that a freelance journalist was writing a piece about the Greenland Missing Persons desk, he did his very best to thwart it, even sending me on two weeks of prisoner escort duty, to get me out of the capital. Of course, he hadn't realised that the journalist was writing the article for *Suluk*, Air Greenland's in-flight magazine, and we met at the airport at the start of my prisoner escort duties.

"Actually, it was your commissioner who let me know where you'd be," the journalist told me over coffee in Nuuk's tiny Arctic airport.

"Really?"

"Yes," he said, with a theatrical turning of the pages of his spiral-bound notebook. "He speaks very highly of you."

I thought of Atii Napa, my long-suffering girlfriend from the academy, the second my cheeks started to flush. She would have teased me about it, together with a comment or two about the young journalist's looks. Of course, if she had been there, during the interview, she might even have given me a few pointers as to how to respond. Atii often acted as my mirror during those moments when a man flirted with me, teasing me at how obvious it was, and questioning just how I could be so oblivious of it. She was usually right. While I might blush at a few compliments, I often needed the sledgehammer approach when it came to picking up on a man's underlying intentions.

And yet, at the crowded table in the airport waiting lounge, the journalist had enough trouble prying the story out of me, let alone asking me for dinner – if that was even his intention.

"I've been lucky," I said, as my cheeks cooled, and my usual skin colour paled to a light creamy brown, typical among many of my fellow Greenlanders, but not all, as European blood was a big part of many Greenlanders' DNA. "The commissioner is very supportive."

"Putting you – a newly graduated constable – in charge of the Greenland Missing Persons department."

"*Desk*," I said, correcting him. "A very small one."

I was tempted to let him write about the *department*, if only to enjoy the sight of Sergeant Duneq's generous jowls quivering with rage. The fact that I, a lowly constable fresh out of the academy, had a dusty desk with a broken chair irked him beyond all reason, but having a whole department… I let the thought linger, like a delicious morsel deliberately left on the side of one's plate, something I could enjoy later, when flying to yet another town to escort yet another prisoner from one jail to another.

"But you are responsible for investigating cases about missing persons in Greenland?"

"I answer the phone," I said.

"Oh, I think you do a little more than that, Constable."

I glanced at the passengers sitting beside us as the journalist checked his notes. With such a small population, Greenlanders shared a strange sense of polite intimacy. It didn't mean that we were entitled to know each other's business, but more often than not we did, if only because of the many threads and personal relations connecting the people across the country. Even so, it could be embarrassing at times, and I spared a mental thanks for whoever had issued me with an overly large police jacket with the stiff collar, behind which I could dip my head.

"You looked for a boy in Qaanaaq?" the journalist said.

"Yes."

"And, more recently, you were involved in a search for a girl in Kangaamiut."

"That's right."

"Two cases, both involving children. Is that typical of a missing persons case in Greenland?"

"I think it was coincidence," I said.

"The boy was missing for nearly a year, and the girl for about three days."

"Yes," I said, frowning as I tried to anticipate his follow-up question.

"And you needed help, in both cases."

"I coordinated with the local police each time."

"Right, but that's not what I meant," he said.

I knew it wasn't. I could see his notes, and there were too many of them scribbled beside the names of the people who had helped me, and far too many question marks for him to ignore them.

"Tell me about Tuukula," he said.

"He lives in Qaanaaq, with his daughter."

"Luui?"

"Yes," I said, smiling at the thought of Luui's tangle of wild black hair, and the freckles striped across her button nose. "She's five."

"And Tuukula helped you in Qaanaaq?"

"They both did."

"And again, in Kangaamiut. But that time…" The journalist paused to check his notes. "You asked for Tuukula's help." He looked up and smiled. "Is he a police consultant?"

"I don't speak Greenlandic," I said, wondering just how much I should reveal about Tuukula's role in my investigations. "He translates for me."

"So, he's a translator?"

"No," I said. "He's a shaman." The word slipped out, before I could stop myself.

"I see," the journalist said, but I could tell that he didn't. The bemused look he wore complemented the look on the faces of the passengers sitting beside us.

"It's complicated," I said, by way of an explanation. "Tuukula seems to be in the right place at the right time, and his daughter…"

"Yes?"

I bit my lip, wishing I hadn't brought Luui into it. It was difficult enough for *me* to appreciate her role in each investigation, and nigh on impossible for strangers to grasp. I settled on one truth, while ignoring the more challenging aspect of her uncanny ability to *see* things that the adults around her missed.

"Luui is quite the charmer," I said. "She disarms people. No," I said, shaking my head as the journalist added to his notes, "that's not the right word. I should have said she puts them at ease."

"And her father? Apart from translating, does he put people at ease too, or does he have other skills that help you solve missing persons cases?"

I had to pause for a moment, as I wondered how to frame my response. The couple next to me leaned in, ever so slightly, as if they were just as eager for the answer as the journalist. I could have embellished Tuukula's role of translation, but at the risk of making a joke of the Greenland Missing Persons desk, I didn't want to ignore his practical skills as a hunter, and the supernatural intuition of the shaman.

"Tuukula is…"

"Yes?"

It was harder than I imagined to put my finger on what he did or didn't do, that helped each case. If Luui had been there, she might have bunched her tiny hand into a small fist, before exploding her fingers with a *poof*, followed by the English word *magic*.

Magic.

There was plenty to be found in Greenland, but the rational and professional part of my mind kicked in, and I remembered the benevolence of Police Commissioner Lars Andersen and I owed it to him and my colleagues to maintain a positive image of the police in Greenland.

"Tuukula is my translator, and my guide in

areas unfamiliar to me."

"Like the spirit world?" the journalist asked, prying.

"Greenland," I said, as my flight was announced over the loudspeaker. "Thank you, but I have to go."

"Just a second," he said, as he pulled out his smartphone. "I need a photo for the article."

As soon as he had taken the photo, I pushed my chair back from the table, and then joined the queue of passengers waiting to board the De Havilland Dash 7 bound for Tasiilaq on Greenland's east coast. Sergeant Duneq planned for me to return that same day, before flying north to Ilulissat and then on to Uummannaq. The journalist promised that I would be able to read a shorter version of his article online by the end of the day.

"It's a teaser for the main piece," he said, as he caught up with me in the queue. "Just to get people interested. It'll be in all three languages, of course. Online and in print in Greenlandic, Danish and English."

"English?"

"You do speak English?" he asked.

"Yes," I said. "It's just Greenlandic that I struggle with."

"Which is why you need Tuukula?"

He was fishing for one last quote, that last piece of magic. But even though I could clearly see and hear Luui saying the word in my mind, I did little more than smile and nod farewell, before stuffing my hands into my jacket pockets and walking to the gate.

CONSTABLE PETRA JENSEN 1-3

They had promised snow later in the week, but even a city girl like me could see that it was already on its way. I patted my pockets to check that I hadn't lost my essentials including my toothbrush, phone charger, a couple of Mars bars, and extra sanitary pads – things I would need if stranded away from home – and then walked the short distance to board the plane.

The commissioner might have spoiled Duneq's plans to stop the interview, but I was still stuck on a flight going east, with the very real threat of being stranded in an airport if the storm caught up with me. I slipped my earbuds into my ears as soon as I found my seat, tuning into my current playlist as the stewardess seated the remaining passengers.

"Magic," I said, as the slow beat of Coldplay's song filtered into my ears.

2

The weather was better in Tunu, the Greenlandic name for the east coast of Greenland. I blinked in the sun as it reflected off the snow, chatting with the airport staff, while we waited for the helicopter from Tasiilaq, the largest town on the east coast. With a population of just over two thousand residents, it was nine times smaller than Nuuk, a fact that always made me smile. It was no secret amongst our friends and colleagues that Atii and I dreamed of living in a big city, and that we thought of Nuuk as the first step before somewhere bigger such as New York or London. Sure, Copenhagen was another option, but I had my sights set further afield.

The shudder of the rotor blades pressing against the airport windows tugged me out of conversation and back into work mode, as I prepared to receive my prisoner for the flight back to Nuuk. Even by Greenlandic standards, Tikaajaat was considered a petty criminal, an opportunist. But it seemed that, lately, he had exploited a long string of opportunities and the locals were tired of him. As Tasiilaq fell under the same municipality as Nuuk, I was tasked with bringing Tikaajaat to the capital, in part to relieve Tasiilaq of his problematic behaviour, but also to spare him from potential harm as his family, his neighbours, and even the people he used to call friends, turned against him. The black eye he wore, together with his limp, suggested that the time was right, that he had received a lesson, but that his teachers had yet to punish Tikaajaat further, as so often happened in the small Greenlandic communities.

"I'm not innocent," Tikaajaat said in Danish, as he buckled into the window seat of the return flight to Nuuk.

"You mean you're guilty?"

"*Iiji*," he said, with a vigorous nod of his small head. "Very."

I hid a smile as he started to list his sins, tapping his fingers for each crime of theft, including stealing alcohol, bullets, money, and cigarettes.

"And one pair of underpants," he said.

"Underpants?"

I'm not sure if I was supposed to talk to Tikaajaat while he was in my custody, but the flight was practically empty and, sitting at the very back of the aircraft, the drone of the Dash 7's four propellers prevented any of the other passengers from hearing what Tikaajaat had to say.

"Worn once," he said.

"The underpants?"

"*Iiji*."

"And you took them?"

Tikaajaat shrugged. "It was cheaper and easier than cleaning my own."

"Right," I said, stifling another smile.

I took a moment to look at Tikaajaat, trying to see past his black eye, the tangle of black greasy hair plastered slick and sweaty on his forehead, his chipped and broken teeth. I wanted to see *him*, if only for a moment, to try to understand what might compel a young man to steal a pair of underpants. My dreams of New York were interrupted by the thought that life in Nuuk – rather, *my* life in Nuuk, was easier in so many ways than Tikaajaat's life in Tasiilaq. I had a regular income – and a good one, by many standards. I had a modern flat, and friends to pick me up when I was down. And yet, it was still possible to see something of myself in Tikaajaat's deep brown eyes, to remember that as a young girl, I had also stolen things – small things, the kind that made a big difference. As a teenager, I had often railed against the rules of the Children's Home, but maybe those rules, and a roof over my head, had been the difference between who Tikaajaat was and who I had become.

"How old are you?" I asked.

"Twenty-three."

We were the same age.

Tikaajaat chatted all the way from Kulusuk to Nuuk, slurping two cups of creamy coffee, and one can of coke. I gave him my cellophane-wrapped biscuit, curious at the care with which he opened it, pressing a wet fingertip to collect the crumbs from the corners of the wrapper. I remembered the bar of chocolate in the cargo pocket on my uniform trousers and pressed it into Tikaajaat's hands. The look he gave me, before he opened it, was just a little too much for me, and I turned away, calling the stewardess to ask for more coffee, in an attempt to hide a sudden swirl of pity surging through my body.

While Sergeant Duneq – *Jowls*, as I called him – might be the bane of my police life, I couldn't help but wonder if, in his own way, he was just trying to toughen me up, and escorting Tikaajaat back to Nuuk was just one more opportunity for me to learn even more about my people.

Tikaajaat slept beside me, his head pressed on my shoulder, and I said nothing more until we landed, rousing him gently before the wheels thudded into the runway.

"Good luck," I said to Tikaajaat, as I handed him over to my colleagues waiting with the patrol car outside the airport.

"You're not coming back to the station?" said Constable Kuno Schmidt, raising his voice over the wind. The Danish police officer blinked in the light snow flurrying across the car park.

"No," I said. "I have to fly north for the next one. Duneq's orders."

"North?" Schmidt pointed at the grey snow clouds pressing in from the sea. "You'll get stranded up there, if you even get that far."

"I think that's part of Duneq's plan." I tried to smile, but the wind caught my hair. I clawed it from my face, waved at Tikaajaat in the back seat, and then jogged back to the airport building. The wind was coming from the south – a strong tailwind to push us north. *We'll make good time,* I thought. *If we leave now.* The flight was boarding, and I joined the queue of passengers, their heads swivelling as they swapped glances with each other, nodding at the weather, then shuffling forward, eager to ride ahead of the storm.

3

The flight should have taken the coastal route, making a sharp right-angled landing at Maniitsoq, then flying on to Aasiaat after a short break, before landing at the slightly larger airport of Ilulissat, the gateway to the north. But the wind cupping the tail of the Dash 7 encouraged the pilots to keep going, ignoring the protests of the passengers headed for the two smaller towns on the route, as they adjusted course for Ilulissat. I didn't mind, for two reasons. I was scheduled to fly on from Ilulissat to Qaarsut and then Uummannaq, by helicopter. But if I was going to be stranded – a common occurrence in Greenland – then I'd choose Ilulissat every time. The hotels were bigger and better, and Air Greenland would be footing the bill. With the exorbitant rents in Nuuk, being stranded in a luxury hotel in Ilulissat was almost like a vacation, one that I could afford.

We flew out of the clutches of the storm, leaving the turbulence behind us, and landing in Ilulissat ahead of schedule. Passengers flying further north were encouraged to leave the aircraft first, in order to catch their connecting flights, quashing any secret hopes I might have had about a forced stay in a hotel, as the ground crew hurried us from one Dash 7 to the next.

Painted bright red, with Air Greenland's classic white logo of a star shaped out of spots, the De Havilland Dash 7s were the workhorses of the north. But the cabin wasn't heated, at least not while the passengers were still boarding. I zipped my collar to my chin and curled my small fists inside the cuffs of my jacket, as the leading edge of the storm arrived in Ilulissat. The crew were eager to take off, and I watched as they snapped curt remarks at a group of American tourists bumbling along the aisle, fiddling with bags in overhead lockers, enjoying the moment.

"Please," the stewardess said. "You need to sit down."

"Yeah, yeah, no problem."

The tallest of the men in the group ignored the stewardess as he pressed a soft holdall into the space in the locker.

"We need to take off."

"Why?" he said. "We're ahead of schedule."

"Oh, come on, Hogan," said one of the women in the group. "Just sit down, already."

The man called Hogan turned to look at her, resting his arm on the top of the seat in front of her as she buckled her seatbelt.

"I'll sit just as soon as I'm ready *Georgina*." He grinned as she curled her lips and fiddled with her thick-rimmed glasses.

"The name's *George*, but you know that."

"Of course I do, *Georgina*." He waved away any further comment with a nod to the stewardess. "But these people will just have to wait."

I looked up at the word *people*, wondering if the

American meant the passengers or the crew. Or if he was addressing Greenlanders in general.

"If you'll sit down," the stewardess said, gesturing at the man's seat.

"Where I come from, you'd call me, *Sir*," Hogan said.

He sat down, and I noted the small smile on the woman's lips as her travelling companion was finally seated.

There were seven in the group, and they seemed less distracted by the weather than I imagined tourists would be on their first visit to the Arctic. They dressed appropriately, which also made me wonder how many times they had been to Greenland. But behind the scarves and beneath their fleece hats, each of them seemed to share a certain degree of irritation. But whether it was directed at the weather or each other, was uncertain. I shivered the thought away, slipped my hands out of my cuffs and tightened my seatbelt, as the stewardess made a quick announcement, rattling through three languages.

"Due to turbulence, there will be no refreshments during the flight," she said. "And please, stay in your seats, and do not use the toilet."

"You mean I can't even take a piss?" Hogan said, lifting his head to look at the stewardess. His chair creaked as he leaned back in it.

"No," she said, as the airframe shuddered with the increased pitch of the engines. "No pissing during the flight, *Sir*."

Everyone smiled at that, even the stewardess.

"Fair enough," Hogan said. He turned to laugh

with his friends, catching my eye as he shifted in his seat. "You're a police officer?" he asked.

"Yes," I said.

"So, I guess you're not allowed to piss, either?"

"I guess not."

"That's fair," Hogan said. He nodded once, and then looked forward, tightening his seatbelt as the Dash 7 thundered down the icy runway.

4

We fled from the storm, droning over the black beaches of Qeqertarsuaq, also known as Disko Island. The coastline was hedged with growlers of ice, the black sand hidden by new snow, as if winter knew summer was coming and was unwilling to relinquish its icy grip of the mountains and the land. The sea ice was already patchy, with large floes sliding up the crests of black waves before crashing and splintering into the troughs below. Those passengers who did not mind the storm pressed their faces to the square windows, exchanging looks and letting go of their seats to point during the brief lulls in the waves of turbulence.

The American, Hogan, was not one of them. I watched as he gripped the arms of his chair, muttering under his breath. I was too far away to hear if he was cursing or praying, but as we flew from one turbulent patch of air into another, I didn't think there was much of a difference.

The captain's voice crackled through the speakers and into the cabin. She apologised for the rough weather, explaining how the early start had perhaps not been early enough to escape the storm.

"But the good news," she said, forcing a measure of optimism into her voice, "is that the helicopter is still flying from mainland Qaarsut to the island of Uummannaq. Until further notice, at least."

I looked out of the window at the ice crystals puckering the glass but chose not to say anything. As selfish as it might sound, I wanted to be on the first helicopter to Uummannaq, preferring to be stranded on the island, than in the settlement of Qaarsut.

The captain prepared us for a bumpy landing, and an even bumpier approach, as she dropped the plane into the leeward side of the mountains, hugging the glaciers tonguing their way down the steep granite sides to the black waters of the fjord below. She curved the Dash 7 in a bumpy arc to land into the wind, finding the balance between dipping and lifting the nose to put air under the wings. The chairs around me creaked, and I wondered if the faux leather covering on the seats, and the arms, could cope with the press of nails from anxious fingers. We landed shortly after, and for once I clapped along with the other passengers in praise of a difficult landing smoothly executed.

As soon as the captain parked the aircraft in front of the airport, I was up and in the aisle, making the most of my lack of luggage and, if I was truthful, exercising a little of my police authority to be the first off the Dash and the first into the helicopter. I forgot all about the Americans as I fastened my seatbelt on the bucket seat inside the helicopter, before reaching up to grab a pair of ear defenders for the short flight to the island. The pilot lifted off and into the wind just a few minutes after the last of the passengers was seated.

CONSTABLE PETRA JENSEN 1-3

Chief of Police Torben Simonsen met me at the heliport. His sharp reputation was softer than I expected, as he waved me into the warmth of the dark blue police Toyota, before driving the short distance to Hotel Asiaq, built onto a low ridge of granite overlooking the harbour.

"You might need some things," he said, after asking about my luggage.

I smiled at the thought of *roughing it* in Qaanaaq, how that experience had changed me. Then I patted my pockets, and said, "I have everything I need."

"Enough for a few days? They say the storm will last until at least the end of the week."

"I'll be fine."

"Well, I've got you in the hotel until then. I called Nuuk and spoke with your Sergeant Duneq." Simonsen glanced at me as if to gauge my reaction before continuing. "There was no rush, you know? Iinta, the guy you're supposed to escort to Nuuk, is no problem, when he behaves. We could have kept him another week."

I looked at Simonsen. We had only ever spoken over the phone, and he was older and greyer than I imagined. He was also Danish, one of a number of Danish policemen who had married a Greenlander, turning a summer position into a permanent one. It reminded me of Constable Kuno Schmidt, and I wondered what he was planning to do once his latest temporary position was over.

"Constable?" Simonsen said, as he parked outside the hotel.

"Yes?"

"I lost you for a moment. I was talking about Duneq."

"Sorry," I said. "Duneq's my supervisor. He likes to keep me busy, and, apparently, as far away from Nuuk as possible."

Simonsen turned in his seat. He tapped a cigarette out of its packet as he leaned his shoulder against the window. "Why?" he asked, as he pinched the cigarette between his lips. "What have you done to piss him off?"

"Nothing," I said, only to add, "Everything. Probably."

Simonsen tapped a packet of matches on his thigh as he waited for me to continue. The unlit cigarette wavered slightly between his lips with each breath.

"He might be jealous, or angry at me. It's a little hard to know."

"Because…"

"Because the commissioner gave me a desk and a phone and told me to take care of the missing persons cases."

"Cases?" Simonsen frowned. "Aren't missing persons just a part of regular police work?"

"Yes," I said. "But every now and again someone calls my phone, and the commissioner encourages me to respond."

"You're a constable."

"Yes."

"Newly trained."

I nodded.

"And you have a desk." Simonsen plucked the cigarette from his lips and laughed. "Perfect. I can just picture George's face, every time that phone rings."

"Twice," I said, once Simonsen stopped laughing.

"What's that?"

"There's been two calls, since I was given it. Although, there's a good chance people have called the number before, but no one has ever answered. Until now."

"Until *you*," Simonsen said. He opened the door a crack, then lit his cigarette in the shelter of the cab before getting out of the car. "Let's get you checked in, then I can go home for the evening." Smoke chuckled out of his mouth as he took his first drag on the cigarette, before making another comment about Duneq. "Missing persons cases, eh?" he said, as we walked to the hotel door.

"Yes."

Simonsen took a couple of long drags on his cigarette, extinguished it between his finger and thumb, then opened the door. I corralled my hair as he waved me inside, before greeting the young woman waiting behind the tall reception desk.

"Welcome to Hotel Asiaq," she said. "My name is Niinu Kilimii. How can I help you?"

I liked her already, and even more so when she smiled and said that I was lucky, the helicopter made just two flights from Qaarsut before being grounded at the heliport.

"You could have been stuck in Qaarsut," she said.

"Yes," I said, allowing myself the briefest of smiles at my good fortune. "I'm very lucky."

5

Niinu clacked long, false nails over the keyboard of the hotel computer. They fascinated me, and I flexed my hand to look at my own nails, bitten to within a millimetre of the cuticle. I was too lazy for my nail biting to become a habit, rather I bit them when I noticed them snagging on my jacket zipper or catching wayward strands of my hair as I tucked them behind my ears. Atii was the first to lament not having long nails when we found a rare evening to spend clubbing in Nuuk. There was only one club, but plenty of DJs, and we convinced ourselves that we were *clubbing*, and that we were training for New York, London, maybe even Paris.

"But we'll need longer nails," Atii had said, one night when we were practicing our winged eyeliner. "False ones," she said. "So we can take them off for work."

I laughed at the memory, curious at just how practical we had become in an effort to balance our careers with our personal lives. Niinu heard me laugh and pushed back from the computer desk to find the key to my room. She moved a power screwdriver to one side as she plucked my key from a rack.

"Actually," she said, as she pressed the key into my hand. "You're doubly lucky."

"How so?"

Niinu pointed at a group photo on the wall behind her desk. A younger and slighter Niinu posed in the front of a group of tourists. "They came two years ago, and are due to arrive on the next helicopter," she said, as she leaned on the counter. "They've taken six double rooms, leaving just one unoccupied." Niinu tapped the key in my hand. "We have twenty rooms, but the rest are being refurbished. My *ataata*, the janitor, is very busy."

"Your dad works here too?"

"As did my *anaana*," Niinu said. "Before she died."

"I'm sorry," I said.

"Not your fault. She was sick – too much to drink. Then one night, she fell asleep outside." Niinu shrugged. "It was winter. She died just four metres from the front door."

I caught her eye for just a second, seeing the grief welling there before she turned back to the photo.

"There used to be seven in the group, but one of the men went missing two years ago." Niinu reached out to press the tip of one of her long nails on the face of a short man standing beside her in the photo. "His name was Justin Moon. He was very kind." Niinu looked away for a moment, as if to catch her breath.

"And they're coming back?"

"*Aap*," Niinu said. "They were on the second helicopter to leave Qaarsut. If they hadn't made it, you would have had the whole hotel to yourself."

Niinu paused to look past me as a pair of bright headlights cut through the snow and lit up the reception area. "Here they come now."

I raised my hand to shield my eyes, recognising a few of the passengers who had flown with me from Ilulissat, including the tall man called Hogan, and the woman he called Georgina.

"You're going to be busy checking them in," I said, lowering my hand. "I'll leave you to it."

"Dinner's at seven," Niinu said, as I climbed the steep staircase to the first floor; I could almost see the sheer wall of granite beneath the foundations with each step.

"Thanks," I said.

I found my room at the top of the stairs, the first on the right along a narrow corridor. The Americans bustled through the front door as I turned the key in the lock. I could still hear them as I closed the door and flopped onto the bed. While Hotel Asiaq didn't have the same number of stars as the bigger hotels in Ilulissat, it was, at least, warm and cosy, if not luxurious. The bed was harder than I was used to, and something heavy – shutters or perhaps a door – was banging in the wind. I closed my eyes for a moment, wishing that the few essentials I had packed included earplugs.

I rolled off the bed and onto my feet when my utility belt started to bother me. I curled it onto the desk, then placed my pistol and two spare magazines in the safe. I checked my phone, and realised I had an hour before dinner. Simonsen said I was his last job before he finished for the day, and I was far enough from Nuuk to escape Sergeant

Duneq's clutches.

"I have the evening off," I said, as I plugged my phone into its charger.

The storm whipped itself into a frenzy outside, scratching the window with needles of ice. The banging continued with a regularity that I knew would keep me awake the whole night, but I discovered that the bathroom was better insulated, and I shrugged off my uniform to take a shower. I didn't have a change of clothes, but I could at least try to dress for dinner. I amused myself with the various ways I could make the light blue shirt of my uniform at least a tiny bit more casual, only to shriek and forget all about it under the first burst of cold water from the shower. It seemed I wasn't the only one freshening up before dinner.

6

It struck me, as I climbed down the stairs for dinner, that the man in the photo had gone missing, but I had not asked *where*. I pushed the thought to one side as the noise from the dining room breached the swing door. I paused before entering, fixing my damp hair into a ponytail, tucking my shirt into my cargo trousers, and affecting as casual a look as I could before dinner. Technically I was off duty, but a police officer is never off, and definitely not when they are still in uniform. It was all still new to me, and Sergeant Duneq hadn't exactly been forthcoming with the grey areas of police work. I think he preferred that I stumble upon them all by myself. I took a breath, pushed the door open, and stepped into the dining room.

"Constable," the man called Hogan said, as I walked to an empty table by the window. "Join us, please."

"Yes, do," said the woman sitting beside him. She tugged at the empty chair next to her, gesturing for me to sit down once she had pulled it out from under the table. "You must join us," she said, as I started to protest. "You can put us girls in the majority for once."

I glanced at the table, blushing under the sudden scrutiny of six strangers, but noting at the same time that the sexes were evenly represented.

"If you're sure?" I said.

"Sure?" Hogan laughed as he reached for the bottle of wine. "*Sure,* we're sure," he said, as he filled a spare glass to the brim. He handed it to me as soon as I sat down. "Unless you're on duty?"

"Sort of," I said, without really being sure. I took a sip as they started the introductions.

"I'm Jordan Carmichaels," said the woman beside me. "I'm a dietician, but you just eat whatever you like, honey, I'm on holiday."

"Which is just as well," Hogan said. "Otherwise she'd be charging by the hour."

"Ignore him," Jordan said. She placed a cool and jewelled hand on mine as she pointed a slender finger at the rest of the group in turn. "Opposite you is Bradley…"

"Washington," the man said, extending his hand across to the table.

I shook it awkwardly with my left hand as Jordan refused to release my right. Greenland has such a small population, with a proportionate diversity. Although Greenland swelled with tourists each summer, Bradley was one of the few black men I had met in person. He smiled at my awkward handshake, before dipping his head towards Jordan as if he understood she was never letting go.

"I'm a contractor," he said, as he let go of my hand.

"What kind?" I asked.

"He builds condos, honey," Jordan said. "Terribly boring."

"But lucrative," Bradley said.

"Of course it is," Hogan said, reaching for the wine. "Especially when they burn down, and you reap the…"

"Hogan!" Jordan said. She patted my hand. "Just ignore him, honey."

Hogan seemed to be the life of the party, or at least, the loudest among them. He was difficult to ignore, and even more so in his loud Hawaiian shirt. My uniform blues paled in comparison. But I wasn't the only one wearing a uniform of sorts. The man sitting beside Hogan wore what looked like a one-piece sleeping suit.

"That's Mosaic," Jordan said, lowering her voice as she pointed at the slim man in the one-piece. "He's our celebrity."

"I can hear you, Jordan," Mosaic said. He wrapped his thin fingers around a tall wine glass, extending his little finger as he took a sip. "Just because *you* don't approve."

"Some of us work for a living," Jordan said. "That's all."

"I work."

"Mosaic, you dear, sweet thing." Jordan lifted her finger, cutting him off as he started to speak. "*YouTubing* is not working. Let's not fight about this again."

"I'm not fighting. I never fight, *Jordan*," Mosaic said. He turned his hand to point his little finger at her. "You start it, every time. Always you. And especially in front of strangers."

Mosaic looked at me, and I blushed again, wishing I had taken the table by the window.

"The Constable…" Jordan paused to squeeze

my hand. "What's your name, honey? We can't call you *Constable* all evening."

"Petra," I said.

"Petra? Such a lovely name." Jordan smiled, before turning back to Mosaic. "Petra is hardly a stranger. *We* are the strangers. This is *her* country, after all."

"And yet here we are, again."

I turned to look at the woman sitting beside Bradley, noting her strong hands, and the square cut of her jaw.

"Let's not get into that," Jordan said.

The woman gave Jordan a look, and I felt the slightest shift in Jordan's grip on my hand, as if the look unsettled her.

"This is Claudia," Jordan said. She let go of my hand to reach for a glass of water.

"Claudia Nickel," the woman said. "Carpenter."

"And I'm a dentist," Hogan said. The table wobbled as he reached across it to shake my hand. "Hogan Mayflower, like the ship," he said.

"The ship?" I said, once he let go of my hand.

"Yes, *the* ship, the pilgrims' ship." He turned to the woman he called Georgina for support. "She doesn't know the ship."

"Not everyone has to know our history," Georgina said. "Do you know the history of Greenland, Hogan?"

"Tiny country, with a population that can fit inside a stadium – why should I?"

"My point, exactly," Georgina said. She turned to me and smiled. "As Jordan said, you should probably just ignore Hogan. God knows we try to."

"And what do you do?" I asked, keen to keep the conversation going, if only to avoid having to talk about Greenland's history, or the *Mayflower*'s.

"I'm a veterinarian," she said. "Which makes me wonder, what can you tell me about the dogs?"

"Dogs?"

"Yes, the sledge dogs." Georgina made a brief sweeping gesture with her hand that seemed to encompass the whole island. "Dotted about the rocks, running free…"

"They're everywhere," Mosaic said.

"Right," Jordan said. "You're a dog person now?"

"Friends," Bradley said. He cleared his throat, then paused to answer a call on his mobile, thumbing the screen to end it as soon as he saw the number. "A toast." The table hushed as everyone reached for their glass. I lifted mine, casting another longing glance at the empty table by the window. "To our new friend, Petra," he said, with a nod in my direction. "And to Justin, our long-lost and sorely missed friend."

"Justin," everyone said, before taking long sips of white or red wine.

"Maybe one day we'll finally discover what happened to him," Bradley said, as he set his wine glass on the table.

"Why not," Hogan said.

"Why not *what*, Hogan?" Jordan said.

"Let's find out what happened to him."

"How?"

"Isn't it obvious?" Hogan pushed his seat back and stood up. "Look," he said, gesturing at me. "We have a detective among us."

"I'm just a constable," I said, only to be drowned out by another burst of Hogan's enthusiasm.

"And the storm," he said, as he walked to window. "It's perfect. Don't you see?"

"See what?" Bradley said.

"That all the pieces of the puzzle are here." Hogan straightened both arms and pointed at the table. "Justin went missing here, and we've been coming back all these years, just hoping there might be a shred of a clue that might tell us what happened." He pointed at the window. "It was a night just like this one. A storm – maybe even stronger and colder than this. I don't remember. But if she can help us, guide us through it."

"Me?" I said, pressing a quick-bitten finger to my chest.

"Yes, Detective. You."

"I don't…"

"Never mind that," he said, waving his hand. "If everyone agrees, then that's what we'll do, now, this very evening. Right after dinner."

"Do what, exactly?" Jordan asked.

"Find Justin's killer."

I swore beneath my breath as the table erupted in curses and accusations. Words such as *stupid* and *immature* crossed back and forth, together with *insensitive* and a longer tirade from Jordan appealing for everyone to calm down and to just ignore Hogan.

The problem was, I couldn't, but it had less to do with being a police officer, and far more to do with my own curiosity. Why else would six barely amicable adults return to the last place they had seen their friend if not to find answers? Perhaps my dinner attire was appropriate after all.

"I'll do it," I said.

"What?" Jordan waved her hands, shushing everyone until she was the only one speaking. "What did you say, honey?"

"I said I'll do it. I'll help you."

"See?" Hogan clapped his hands together. "Perfect. We'll start straight after dinner."

7

Hotel Asiaq had a study, although the name of the room was perhaps grander than the room itself. The mahogany veneer panels screwed into the walls, together with a classic American library style lamp, complete with brass fittings and a jade shade, added a touch of old-world class, wholly out of place in Greenland, but not unpleasant. The floorboards creaked as I squeezed around the desk, and the ornaments on the shelves – *Tupilaq* carved out of narwhal teeth and whale bone – rattled within a millimetre of toppling. The dust on the shelves suggested that few people visited the study, but it was perfect for my purpose.

"What are you going to do?" Niinu asked.

"I'm going to help the group discover what happened to their friend – the one you showed me in the photo."

"And why... I mean *how* are you going to do that?"

"By asking lots of questions."

"Is this a case then?" Niinu's forehead creased as she frowned.

"Not really," I said, wondering how I should describe it. "I suppose you could call it evening entertainment."

"Oh," Niinu said. "That's better."

"Why?"

"Because I don't think the Chief would be happy if you were investigating. *Ataata* said he was quite frustrated."

"Because they never found Justin?"

"*Aap*. It was the month of May and we still had sea ice, so there were no boats on the water. The ice was getting thin, and the police had just said we couldn't drive on it anymore. Then Justin disappeared, and the Chief was pissed off that he might have gone for a walk. They had hunters out searching the ice, and then the Chief sent one of his officers up the mountain." Niinu turned to point in the direction of the heart-shaped mountain that loomed over the town of Uummannaq.

"But they didn't find any clues?"

Niinu shook her head.

"Not a trace?"

"Nothing."

The fine hairs on my arms prickled with a surge of excitement as I teased at Niinu's memory of what happened to Justin Moon. I didn't want to step on Simonsen's toes, but as long as the case was nothing more than entertainment, a way to pass the time during the storm, I decided that I could go ahead. I tugged my smartphone out of my pocket and slid it onto the desk.

The study was tucked into a corner of the hotel, close to the kitchen. I wouldn't have been surprised if it used to be a pantry, before being remodelled as a feature for the hotel. Once Niinu had gone, and if I didn't move, the study was silent, but the storm outside sifted snow along the outer walls like sand,

and from somewhere outside, I could hear the same shutter banging in the wind.

I looked up as Jordan knocked on the door.

"Can I come in?"

"Yes, of course," I said.

Jordan took a moment to glance around the study, turning her head to the bone figures as they rattled on the bookshelves.

"I just wanted to ask if you're okay with this?"

"I am," I said.

"Only, Hogan can be so bullish at times. Some people find it hard to say no to him."

"It's okay. Really."

Jordan cupped her hands in front of her, resting them just above the slim belt of her jeans. She turned the largest of her rings on her left hand with the little finger of her right, turning the ring back and forth as she looked at me.

"Was there something else?" I asked. "Would you rather I didn't do this?"

"What?"

"Am I being insensitive?"

My excitement diminished as I realised I probably was. The combination of being stranded by bad weather, trapped in a hotel on a remote island, and presented with a true missing persons case had diluted my better judgement. I thought briefly of Tuukula, almost expecting him to appear in the doorway, teasing me with a knowing smile, waiting for me to come to my own conclusion about my next step, or the best course of action.

"No, of course not. Everything is fine," Jordan said. "It's all fine, honey." She paused to look at her hands, then held them by her sides, as if suddenly self-conscious about her ring-turning. "To be honest, I think we all want to know what happened to Justin, but…" She laughed. "You saw us at dinner. We're not good at talking. We're far too combative, I think."

"But you want to know what happened to Justin?"

"Yes. Absolutely. That's why we came back."

Jordan looked at me for a moment, then looked away, before excusing herself, and promising to send someone in to begin.

"Who would you like, first?" she asked.

I hadn't thought about it.

"How about Hogan?" Jordan said. "After all, he started it. He might as well go first."

"That's fine," I said. "I'll find a second chair."

Jordan nodded, then slipped out of the study. I followed her out, stopping in the dining room to find another chair. When I returned, I found Hogan sitting behind the desk.

"So, Detective," he said, lacing his fingers behind his head. "Shall we begin?"

8

"Justin was an ass," Hogan said. He spun my smartphone on the desk between us, drawing my attention to his thick fingers, and making me wonder how a dentist with such big hands could do work inside small mouths. Hogan, however, had a big mouth, and lots of opinions. I said nothing. I just let him speak.

"Don't get me wrong, he was a great guy, but he was a real pain in the ass." Hogan stopped spinning my phone and leaned back in the chair. He ran his thick fingers through his greasy blond hair a couple of times before continuing. "Everybody loved him, of course we did. But he had this way about him, no matter how you talked with him, he just had this kind of expectant manner. I don't know how to describe it, but he would pause – you know? He'd say something and then pause, as if you had to fill in the blank. Like he *expected* you to do it. I guess it had something to do with his job. He was an insurance broker. Did I mention that?"

"No."

"He was good at it. He had a successful business, writing policies to fit people's needs, and I mean exactly. Say you had an expensive watch."

Hogan reached forward, pressing his hand close to my face and turning it so that I could see the big gold watch on his wrist. He pulled it back and wiped a speck of imaginary dust from the face.

"You have something like this, you want to insure it, believe me. But Justin could write a policy that was so specific, tailor-made, if you know what I mean?"

"Yes," I said, but it was unnecessary. Hogan continued without even glancing at me.

"So, this watch – I know it has a dodgy winder. Too thin for my fingers. So, I asked Justin if he could write a policy that allowed me to claim for the watch, if it was stolen, or broken, but also to claim for the winder. It breaks all the time, but the deductible – you know, what you pay before the insurance coverage kicks in?"

I nodded.

"Well, Justin wrote a policy that covered the winder. I mean, I'm breaking it all the time. So, he does one of his expectant pauses, like I just told you about, and he waits, and I ask him if he could write me something that lets me claim on the winder? I love this watch. It was my grandfather's. But if I had to pay to get it fixed every time the winder broke; I may as well buy a new watch. Justin helped me out with that. Sure, the premium is a little higher, but the number of times I break the winder… Let's just say it works out for me in the end. He did the same thing with policies for my practice." Hogan paused. "And George's dog."

"George?"

"Yeah, Georgina. She likes to be called George. I think it's because she's from the east coast, New York state."

"But you call her Georgina," I said.

"Sure, to her face. That's right. But, hey, it's just you and me, Detective."

Hogan grinned and added one of what he might describe as Justin's expectant pauses. I filled it with a question about George – or Georgina's – dog.

"What kind of policy?"

"For her dog?" Hogan nodded once more. "She's got an Afghan. It sheds," he said, shaking his hand. "It sheds so much, it's like it's got a disease or something. So George insured the dog's fur. I mean, that's how good Justin was. You'd think brokers would write an insurance policy for anything. But that's just a load of bull. But Justin? He actually did it." Hogan paused to take a long breath. "He insured everything. I guess that, at the end, he might have insured too much."

"I don't understand," I said. "How could he insure too much?"

"Did I say that?" Hogan glanced at my phone.

"Yes."

"Right, okay. Maybe someone asked him to insure something he shouldn't have. What do I know? You'd have to ask the others."

Hogan rested his hands in his lap, then looked away, commenting on the ugly faces of the *Tupilaq* on the shelves as I puzzled over what he had said about insurances. I decided to leave it and return to the basic details I needed to piece together the events surrounding Justin's disappearance.

"Justin went missing two years ago," I said. "What happened that night?"

"You mean what do I remember?"

"Yes, whatever you can. Anything will help. And if you know what you told the police…"

"The police?"

"Yes," I said. I could feel what Atii called my curious frown pinching the skin just above my nose. "The chief of police, Simonsen. Niinu told me he organised a search."

"For Justin?"

"Yes."

"I don't remember anyone doing any searching." Hogan shook his head. "Justin just disappeared. He was at dinner. He sat next to Mosaic, I think. They talked. We all talked. We all drank a bit – maybe too much. It was the last night before we flew the following morning."

"And the next morning?"

"I had a really thick head. A hangover, you know?"

"Yes," I said. I knew all about hangovers, but the way Hogan fidgeted on the chair as he talked was far more interesting.

"We got a ride to the heliport. I remember asking where Justin was. It was me who asked," he said, leaning close to my phone. "But no one had seen him at breakfast. And then we had to go."

"So, you just left him?"

"Hey, we're all adults here. It's not like we're family. Sure, someone must have knocked on his door. Maybe Jordan. I don't know. But then we had to go, and you know what it's like. When the weather is right, you just have to go. You can't wait around. It might be sunny one minute, and a real storm the next." He turned in his seat, looking for a window, only to point at the bookshelf when he realised there wasn't one.

"You left together?"

"In the hotel car. Two trips."

"Without Justin?"

"Hey, I asked where he was. If anyone had seen him. Then we just had to go."

"And the last time you saw him?"

"He was sitting next to Claudia at dinner."

"Claudia?"

"That's right." Hogan pointed at my phone. "Check your recording. That's what I said."

It wasn't, and he knew it. But before I could quiz him about it, he pushed back his chair and walked out of the study.

9

As Hogan left the study, the wind outside filled the void, together with the flap and bang of the shutter somewhere below the study. The hotel was built on thick wooden stilts on top of the rocks, just like all the houses on the island. Some of the houses had plywood sheets screwed into the stilts to make a cellar of sorts, albeit of various sizes and degrees of functionality. Mostly, it was to improve the aesthetic look of a house. In the case of the hotel, the name was painted in large white letters along the plywood façade facing the harbour. Access to the Arctic cellars was often through a small door or hatch, and I could just imagine that the wind had teased one of the hatches open. I thought about looking for it, but Mosaic stopped me as I stood up to leave the study.

"You're leaving?" he said. "I can come back."

"No, it's fine," I said, gesturing to the seat Hogan had just vacated. "Please sit down."

"I suppose you want to know all about me?" Mosaic said.

I waited for him to sit down, intrigued by the way he brushed the seat of the chair with the cuff of his shirt before sitting.

"A little, I guess," I said.

"You don't have *YouTube* in Greenland? Is it

blocked?" Mosaic leaned over the desk as I started a new recording. "Are you living under an oppressive regime?" he whispered.

"Greenland is a democracy," I said, wrangling the smile from my lips.

"Sure, I knew that, but you hear all kinds of things. And I just wanted to be sure you were okay."

I felt the brush of soft cotton on my skin as Mosaic reached out to pat my hand. His fingers were hidden inside his cuffs.

"If you could just tell me about your relationship to Justin. How you knew him. Maybe how you met."

"How we met?" Mosaic smiled, flashing a set of perfect teeth. "He insured my teeth. And in my work, *that's* a serious investment. Oh, sure, you can do wonders with lighting and editing. But video is just one medium. I like to meet people."

"And is Hogan your dentist?"

"That pig?" Mosaic sneered. "God no. I wouldn't trust him to work on a mannequin. Have you seen his hands?"

"Yes," I said, wondering if I shouldn't have said anything at all.

"Never mind that. Justin insured my teeth. He put me in touch with Jordan. She told me what to eat, so that I wouldn't colour my teeth. You noticed I drank the white wine, not the red? Just like I don't drink coffee or tea."

"But at dinner, I got the impression that you and Jordan…"

"We're on a break," he said. "Too much of a

good thing, I think. We need a pause. That's all."

"And Justin?"

"That night, two years ago, everything changed."

I caught a glimpse of Mosaic's hands as he rested his elbows on the table and propped his chin between laced fingers. Unlike my lazy approach to biting nails, it seemed that Mosaic was a connoisseur, and that he chose his long-cuffed shirts with care. But as he recalled the last night he had seen Justin, it seemed that the insurance broker's disappearance was of greater concern than revealing the quicks of his fingers.

"I liked Justin," he said. "And he knew it."

"You had a relationship with him?"

"Oh, please," Mosaic said, with a shake of his head. "I said I liked him, but I was never going to *love* him. You understand?"

"I think so."

"Justin *loved* everybody. And I just didn't have the time for that kind of thing. I let him know that I was available, but that I wasn't going to wait, and that he would have to stop sleeping around if he wanted to have anything, and I mean *anything* to do with me."

Mosaic slipped his fingers back inside his cuffs as he leaned back in his chair.

"Was Justin in a relationship?" I asked. "With any of the others in your group?"

"Our *group*?" Mosaic laughed. "It's not like we're a band. We don't *group*. Although, Justin had his groupies. Just ask Bradley."

"Justin had a relationship with Bradley?"

"I didn't say that. But if I did say that, or if I was saying anything like that, I would say that you had to ask Bradley where he was the night Justin disappeared. That's all I'm saying."

"Where were you the night he disappeared?"

"Me?" Mosaic shrugged. "I was at dinner. Then I took a walk with Jordan – you can ask her."

"I thought there was a storm?"

"Oh, sure," he said. "We just took a short walk, just outside the door really. One last cigarette."

"Cigarettes stain your teeth," I said, feeling another pinch of curiosity above my nose.

"You've got a smart mouth, Detective." Mosaic's lips curled as he spoke. "But sure, you're right. That's why it was our *last* cigarette." He paused to point at my phone. "Are you recording this?"

"Yes."

"Then you'll have to sign something – a disclaimer. I sell everything. My image, my voice. I'll need a chit to prove you won't try and sell that."

"It's just for my notes."

"Whatever. I'll still need a chit."

Mosaic stood up and walked to the door. I stopped him with a last question.

"Did you knock on Justin's door, the next morning?"

"What?"

"You had to be at the heliport. I understand the hotel car was going to take you."

"And?"

"You were leaving as a group. If Justin wasn't there…"

"Oh, sure, I knocked on his door." Mosaic shrugged. "He said he was getting ready, and that we should just go on without him."

"What time did he say that?"

"The time?" Mosaic lifted his hands and let his cuffs roll down his pale arms. "I don't wear a watch," he said, letting his hands fall to his sides. "But it was after breakfast. That I remember." He took a last glance at my phone, and said, "I'll still need that chit."

10

My head buzzed with Hogan and Mosaic's slightly different account – just enough to confuse me, with plenty to pique my interest. It seemed strange that at least two of the group were unaware that the police had searched for Justin Moon on the day they left the island. Even more curious, was the fact that although they professed to be friends, they showed little sympathy when he missed his flights – the helicopter to the mainland, and the fixed-wing flying south for their connecting flight home.

But why Greenland?

Tourists rarely came more than once to Greenland, the cost of flights, food and accommodation were prohibitive. But seven Americans visited Greenland, and the same group came back two years following the death of one of their group. It seemed clear to me that finding a motive for their visit was crucial to understanding how or why Justin might disappear.

I thought of Atii and wished she were with me, although mysteries had never been her thing.

"Mysteries are for lawyers," she once said during training. "I don't mind gathering information and passing it on, but when I go home at night, I just want to relax, not sit on the couch or lie in bed thinking about stuff. Life's too short for that."

I needed help.

I thumbed the screen of my smartphone to check the time, cursing as I realised it was getting later and later. Simonsen would be home now, and I could hardly disturb him with an emergency, since the missing person had been missing for two years. It would have to wait until morning.

"But I need a break," I said, as I walked out of the study.

The man leaning against the counter in the hotel reception was tall enough to give Sergeant Gaba Alatak a run for his money. I hadn't thought of Gaba for a while – I tried not to. It was hard enough listening to Atii's tales of romantic conquests with the leader of the police Special Response Unit, but, regardless, stray thoughts of Gaba popped into my head whenever I least expected, often prompted by the least expected things.

Like the man in reception.

"Juuliu," he said, offering his hand as I approached. "I'm Niinu's *ataata*." His Danish was flawless, surprising me, as he nodded at the empty chair in front of the computer. "I'm just waiting for her."

"You're the janitor."

"*Aap*," he said. His bushy black eyebrows wriggled as he smiled.

"There's something banging outside," I said.

Juuliu nodded. "I know, but I haven't found it yet."

"I think it's a shutter, or something."

Juuliu reached over the counter to pick up the power screwdriver I had seen earlier. "And when I find it, I'm going to fix it," he said.

"Now?"

"*Imaqa.*" He shrugged, and then looked at his watch. "It's late. Maybe it will blow off in the storm. Then I don't have to fix it."

There was a certain logic to that, and I nodded that it could wait.

"Unless you want to go out and look?"

"Outside?"

"*Aap*," he said. "You look like you need some air."

"Yes," I said. "But I'll need my jacket."

Juuliu moved away from the counter and ducked beneath an arch leading to the kitchen. He returned with a huge *Canada Goose* down jacket, with a fur-lined hood.

"It's Niinu's," he said. "You can borrow it."

"Thanks," I said, as I slipped my arms into the sleeves, and then zipped the jacket all the way to top of the collar. The fur tickled my forehead, and I adjusted the strap at the back of the hood to lift it a little.

"Are we done already?"

I turned my head to one side, looking for whoever spoke, only to have Juuliu grasp my shoulders and turn me back again until I was facing Bradley Washington. Both men were taller than me, and I lifted my chin to look up.

"Mosaic said you were ready for me."

"Yes," I said.

"She's having a break," Juuliu said, surprising me for a second time with his English. "We'll be back soon."

Juuliu steered me towards the front door. I tried to adjust the hood again but gave up in a fit of giggles as I bumped into the glass window beside the door.

"This way," Juuliu said.

"I can't see," I said.

"*Aap*. I know."

We left Bradley in the reception. I might have thought about his reaction, perhaps even promised that I would be back soon, but the wind buffeted me across the icy ground outside the hotel, and the cold choked the breath out of my lungs. Juuliu bent his arm and I hooked my hand around it, following his lead as we slid across the ice and stomped in the snow around the side of the hotel.

I let Juuliu lead as I concentrated my efforts on dipping my head and placing my feet. I bumped into him as he stopped, and then looked up when he tapped my shoulder.

"There," he said, jabbing his bare fingers at a square door banging in the wind.

"Are you going to screw it shut?" I said, shouting into the wind.

"*Aap*."

I let go of Juuliu as he fiddled with the screwdriver in his hands. He cursed as he dropped several long screws into the snow at his feet, and again when he realised the battery was empty.

"I have another battery inside," he said, pressing his face close to my hood. "Do you want to come back with me?"

A gust of icy wind pushed me off balance, and I gripped Juuliu's arm, steadying myself before replying.

"I'll wait here," I said, then pointed at the cellar door. "I'll wait inside."

"You're sure?"

"Yes," I said.

Juuliu nodded once, and then slipped away. I watched him follow the path through the rocks back to the corner of the hotel. As soon as he was gone, I reached for the door, holding it as I peered into the cellar inside. There was a flashlight on my utility belt, and I sighed at the thought of going back to my room to fetch it. But as I peered into the cellar, I noticed a dim light creeping around the corners of more plywood sheets deeper inside the cellar, as if there were two cellars, one inside the other.

The choice was easy. I could stay outside and freeze, or I could crawl inside the cellar and wait for Juuliu to return. The third option of walking back to the hotel didn't even occur to me, I was too curious to leave without at least taking a quick look and checking out the light.

I took a moment to hitch the tails of Niinu's long coat up to my waist, folding and bunching the coat until it was more like a jacket. I cinched the draw cords tight before lifting one leg up and then through the cellar entrance. The door flapped against my shoulder and I worried that a rusty nail might rip Niinu's jacket. But with one leg already inside, I was committed. I crawled the rest of the way in and paused to let my eyes adjust to the dark.

The rocks inside were dusted with snow, and at the back of cellar, lit by the soft glow of light creeping around the sheets of plywood, was a row of three wooden coffins.

11

In any other country, coffins hidden beneath a hotel might have raised alarm bells, if they had been discovered. But in Greenland, an empty coffin was an empty vessel, something to be used. The square door cut into the plywood sheets that created the cellar was too small for the coffins to be removed. So, if they couldn't be used for their original purpose, and they couldn't be moved without breaking them apart, then the only logical thing to be done with them was to use them for storage. Somebody had done just that, sliding the lids to one side to make room for tins of paint inside. I smiled at the practical use of the coffins, before taking a closer look at the plywood sheets boxing the smaller room inside the cellar, out of which a creamy yellow light shone between the joins.

The bottom section of each plywood sheet had been cut like a jigsaw puzzle to accommodate the irregular peaks and mounds of the granite upon which the hotel was built. The sheets were screwed into the thick stilts supporting the hotel above my head. I slipped my hand beneath one ragged edge of plywood and turned it in the light, tilting my head to one side to see around my breath crystallising in the chill cellar air. Niinu's long jacket was surprisingly warm, and the wind did little more than funnel tendrils of dry snow into the cellar, like thin powdery fingers reaching in, questing for something to hold onto.

Together with the flapping of the door, and the darkness, barely broken by the thin rectangles of yellow light, the scene was set for a horror movie, and I pulled my hand out of the light. I unfolded the tails of Niinu's jacket down to my knees and felt something stiff crumple inside one of the pockets. I slipped my hand inside and pulled out an envelope, turning it in the available light to read the address and that of the sender, before admonishing myself for intruding on Niinu's privacy, and stuffing the envelope back into Niinu's pocket.

"Found something interesting?" said a deep voice behind me.

The man's voice, the horror setting, and being caught in the act of looking at someone's private correspondence gave me a start, and I spun around, slipping in the snow until I landed on my backside. Bradley's big frame filled the cellar entrance as he squeezed through the square door. I caught my breath as I watched him, wondering how he could fit, and, if he did, how he might get out again.

"I'm guilty," he said, once he was inside the cellar. "Of following you."

"Why did you?"

He jabbed his thumb towards the roof and nodded. "I was ready for my interview, but you took off."

"I was going to come back."

"I know," he said. "But I was curious, and now we're here I'm even more curious." He pointed to his left. "Are those coffins?"

"Yes," I said.

"Empty?"

"No." Bradley started to shiver as I smiled. "They're full of paint pots and stuff."

"Paint?"

"Yes."

Bradley clenched his fists as he began to shake. "What else do you know? I mean, what did Hogan and Mosaic tell you?"

"I'm not sure I should say," I said. "At least not yet." Bradley started to shiver in his thin jacket and even thinner jeans. "Perhaps we should go. You look cold."

I stood up and took a step towards the square door banging in the wind. Bradley moved to block my path.

"First," he said, teeth clacking. "Tell me what the others said."

"Bradley…"

"Tell me," he said.

He raised his arm, holding out a massive hand as if to push me deeper into the cellar. He lowered it again to wrap his arms around his chest.

"Do I have to remind you I'm a police officer?" I said, but he seemed distracted.

"What's that light?" he asked, looking around me. "What's inside that room?"

"I don't know."

"Those panels have been moved." Bradley shuffled forward to take a closer look at the snow drifting up and beneath the bottom of the panels. "Sawdust in the snow," he said, before pointing at the large flathead screws drilled into the edges of the panels in neat rows. "It's recent. They've been screwed in and out, since it started snowing."

I followed the direction in which Bradley was pointing, wishing for the second time that I had my flashlight. But a closer inspection revealed sawdust sprinkled on top of and down the fresh drifts of snow that the wind had blown along and up the granite floor. There wasn't much, but enough to suggest that it was new.

"Juuliu will know," I said, as I wondered about footprints. I laughed again as I grasped at assumptions, assuming that the sawdust was significant, that something of interest was hidden behind the panels. But the only recent footprints would be my own, Bradley's and Juuliu's, if he had even been down here. The light could have been on for weeks, depending upon the bulb.

I decided it was nothing of interest. Someone had probably turned a light on somewhere and forgot to turn it off. Old hotels like old houses would be full of strange switches, forgotten each time the building changed hands, only to be discovered again by chance, or during a renovation.

But, perhaps, there was more to this light. Juuliu revealed as much when he returned and poked his head inside the square door, looking at me, before flicking his eyes to the light.

The flicker suggested it was not supposed to be turned on.

I wanted to ask Juuliu about the light and the inner cellar, only to be distracted by Bradley as he started to speak, slurring his words as he removed his jacket, I knew any questions I had would have to wait. Bradley Washington was going hypothermic.

12

"You have to help me, Juuliu," I said, as I struggled to zip Bradley's jacket. Each time I got the zip halfway up his jacket, he brushed my hands away, complaining that he was too hot. "I can't do this by myself."

Juuliu was more interested in the light behind the panels. He crawled into the cellar and worked his way towards the inner room.

"Juuliu," I said, tugging at his jacket sleeve. "Bradley needs our help. We have to get him inside." I paused to look at Bradley, noting the deep purple colour of his lips, and adjusted my plan. "He's too far gone," I said, pulling my smartphone from my pocket. "We need to get him to hospital."

Perhaps it was the word hospital that finally convinced Juuliu that one of the guests needed help. He put the screwdriver down, and nodded that he would help, glancing just one more time at the light before helping me guide Bradley to the hole leading out of the cellar.

I had forgotten about the wind.

The square door caught my head as I crawled out of the cellar, dazing me for a moment until the sharp bite of the wind cleared my head and I held the door to one side as Juuliu pushed Bradley's head and shoulders out of the cellar and into the wind. I took Bradley's hands, reminding myself that he was a building contractor as the strength of his grip surprised me.

He spotted the sawdust.

The thought needled one part of my mind, just like the snow spinning through the wind needled my eyes, splintering upon my cheeks. I let go of Bradley for a second to claw my hair out of my eyes but gave up a second later. We had to get him inside. I could worry about my hair later. Juuliu said something about nailing the door shut, but I convinced him that it could wait.

"We have to get him inside, and then call the ambulance."

I fumbled my phone back into my pocket, deciding that getting Bradley inside was the priority. Juuliu nodded, giving the cellar one last glance before supporting Bradley on one side, as I held onto the other. Bradley shivered as we staggered along the path to the hotel entrance, dripping nonsense words from his mouth all the way to the door. Niinu stared at us for a moment from behind the desk, before running to the door to open it.

"Call the hospital," I said to Niinu, as we dumped Bradley into the large armchair by the door. "Tell them he's hypothermic."

Niinu nodded and ran back to the desk. As she started to dial, Bradley's companions drifted out of the dining hall into the reception area.

"What's wrong with him?" Hogan asked.

"He's cold," I said.

"He's cold? We're all cold."

"He was outside," I said, curbing my irritation as I focused on Bradley. Juuliu brought blankets from a cupboard set into a recess in the wall, and we wrapped them around Bradley's shoulders.

"What was he doing outside?" Georgina asked, hushing Hogan as he made another quip about how it was supposed to be cold in Greenland. "I thought he was your next interview?"

"He was," I said.

I paused as the ambulance headlights flashed up the steep slope to the hotel entrance. The driver and one of the porters from the hospital climbed out of the ambulance – a white transit – and then grabbed a wheelchair from the back of the van. It might have been comical, and anyone else might have laughed at the sight of two small Greenlandic men trying to stuff a large American man into a tiny wheelchair, but no one laughed. Neither was anyone watching Bradley as the hospital staff wheeled him through the storm to the back of the ambulance. They were all looking at me.

"And?" Georgina asked, as the driver carefully reversed the ambulance down the slope and back onto the road. "Did you?"

"What?"

"Interview him?"

"No," I said.

"But did he say anything to you?"

I don't know what had changed since I interviewed Mosaic, but the banter around the dining table had changed into a palpable tension, sparking between the guests.

"Maybe we should have some coffee," I said,

catching Niinu's eye. "Then I can tell you what I know so far."

"I think that's a good idea," Jordan said, and she ushered everyone back into the dining room. "Let's give her a moment, and then the detective can bring us up to speed."

"Constable," I said, but they were already gone.

Juuliu said something quietly in Greenlandic to his daughter, before closing the cupboard door and excusing himself. I expected him to go outside, to screw the cellar door shut, but instead he walked to the kitchen.

Niinu stared at me, her eyes fixed on the deep pockets of her jacket.

"I'm sorry," I said. "Juuliu said I could borrow it."

Niinu nodded, but her eyes remained fixed on the pockets.

"I found something. And I'm sorry, but I bent it a little." I tugged the envelope out of the jacket and pressed it into Niinu's hands. "I hope it wasn't important."

"It's just a letter," Niinu said, as she took the envelope from my hand.

She bit her bottom lip, so quickly I almost missed it, and I almost dismissed it. But the one thing I had seen on the envelope was the sender's address: Missouri, USA.

I gave Niinu her jacket and she promised she would arrange the coffee, leaving me with the guests and a list of interviews to be resumed after the break.

As soon as Niinu was gone, I walked to the

dining room, pausing with my hand on the door, cursing my initial enthusiasm as I began to wonder what I had gotten myself into.

13

Everyone spoke at once. Between accusations and insinuations including Hogan's obsession with his watch, Jordan's useless dietary advice, and the suspicious motives surrounding Bradley following *the detective* to the cellar, I took another long and lingering look at the table for two tucked into the alcove of the dining room window. Between flurries of driving snow and the drifts pluming up over the rocks and onto the plates of sea ice jostling between the small fishing cutters in the harbour, there was a sense of calm, so far removed from the storm that raged between the hotel guests. They quietened down as Niinu arrived with a trolley of fresh coffee and a small selection of cakes. Jordan apologised for their behaviour, while Hogan helped himself to more cakes and sugar in his coffee than I imagined a dentist would recommend. But as the heat of their argument settled into a warm exchange of pleasantries about the smell of the coffee and the number of blueberries in the slices of cake, I realised they were waiting for me to say something, so I told them about the coffins.

"In the basement?" Georgina asked.

"Yes," I said, pausing as Niinu dropped a cup onto the floor. She apologised, catching my eye, if only briefly, before excusing herself and hurrying back to the kitchen.

"How many?" Claudia asked.

"Three that I could see," I said. I waited until they were seated before telling them what I knew of coffins in Greenland. It wasn't a lot, but it made a little more sense when I explained that the coffins were old and unused. I didn't mention the paint.

"And you say that carpenters stored the coffins under their houses?" Jordan said.

"Yes." I sat down as Georgina gestured at the chair next to her. "You can't dig graves in the winter," I said.

"Permafrost," Hogan said. "I read about it."

I nodded once, and then again as Jordan offered to pour me a cup of coffee. "So," I said, as she placed the coffee on the table in front of me. "Years ago, the bodies would be kept in the coffins under the carpenter's house, until the ground thawed in the summer and they could be buried."

"Like a mortuary, honey?" Jordan asked.

"More like a chapel," I said.

"Claudia's a carpenter," Hogan said, turning to look at her. "Got any bodies in your basement, Claudia?"

"No," she said. "But you just say the word, and I'll build you a coffin."

"Really?" Hogan snorted. "I bet you'd like that."

"I would," she said. "But only if you've got insurance."

"That's enough, you two," Jordan said. "The detective is just trying to help."

"I'm just a constable," I said, but my words

were lost in another round of squabbling until Mosaic raised his voice, slapping his hand on the table to be heard.

"Hey. People," he said. "Just stop, already. I want to know what Bradley said down in the cellar."

"What he said?" Hogan snorted for a second time. "It doesn't matter what he *said*. It's the fact that he followed the detective down there at all that interests me. I mean, did anyone else know there was a basement?"

"Actually," I said. "It's more like a wall of wood around the rocks."

"Whatever," Hogan said. "I didn't know there was a basement."

"Bradley builds condos," Claudia said. "Of course, he knew there would be a basement. And then he saw her," she said, pointing a thick finger at me. "So he followed her."

"Why?" Mosaic said. "There's a storm. What made him want to follow her so bad he'd go out in a storm? I mean, is he trying to hide something?"

"We don't know that," Jordan said. "And now he's in hospital."

"Right," Mosaic said. "He's the victim now, playing his part." He waved his long cuffs at Hogan as he started to speak, shushing the others with a scowl before he continued. "Does anyone else remember the call Bradley got at dinner? The one from the IRS? He's under investigation. Probably fraud. They found him out."

"Fraud?" I said.

"That's right, *detective*." Mosaic pushed back

from the table and stood up. He made a show of walking to the coffee trolley, drawing out his story as he poured another cup for himself, before generously offering to top up everyone else's, milking the limelight. "Think about it. Those condos that burned down. Remember? Was it coincidence that Justin insured them? I don't think so. And then Justin goes missing. It was Bradley who offered to clean out Justin's office. But I bet none of you ever asked what he was looking for. Did you?"

"What do you mean?" Jordan said. "What was he looking for?"

"Receipts, chits, evidence," Mosaic said, as he walked back to his seat.

I could see it now, the missing link drawing them all together. Each of them knew Justin as an insurance broker first, and a friend – perhaps even a distant friend – second. He connected them.

Hogan cut through a moment of awkward silence with a long, hearty laugh, spilling cake crumbs from his mouth and drawing disgusted looks from Jordan and Georgina. Claudia turned away from him, catching my eye for a moment with what felt like a penetrating stare, as if she was trying to figure out what I knew, or what I might deduce from the talk around the table. She excused herself a second later, grabbing her jacket from the back of her chair and walking across the room.

"Don't forget to talk to the detective," Jordan called out, as Claudia reached the door.

"Whenever she's ready," Claudia said over her shoulder.

CONSTABLE PETRA JENSEN 1-3

My phone rang as she left the dining room, and I retreated to a quiet corner to answer it, smiling at the name of the caller displayed on the screen.

"Hey, Atii," I said, as I answered her call.

"Where are you?"

"Uummannaq."

"Still?"

"I'm stranded, Atii. Stuck here until the storm blows over."

"You poor thing, P. Trapped on an island. What are you doing?"

I paused to look around the room, catching fragments of more arguments, this time about insurance, and who had insured what and for how much.

"I'm working on a missing persons case. I think."

"You think?"

"Yes," I said. "But right now, I'm wondering if it was murder."

14

There are very few murders in Greenland. The majority of violent situations in Greenland usually involved people who knew each other, but rarely did they end in murder. While some of the victims were seriously hurt, there was often something linking them to the person or persons hurting them. In small communities, such violent episodes could sometimes be prevented as the local police and community workers coordinated their efforts to support the families, and to keep an eye on them, especially those families with children. In Tikaajaat's case, they sent him to Nuuk. But even in a country with a gun in almost every house, murder was a rare event.

I finished my call with Atii, promising to stay safe and to keep her updated. I pictured her at home, watching another episode of *Friends*, or something similar, relaxing before her next shift. I thought about the hard bed back in my hotel room and felt a sudden pang of longing for my own bed, my own apartment. I spared an evil thought for Sergeant Duneq, wondering if he had seen the *Suluk* article online, followed by another evil thought that I could leave a copy of the in-flight magazine in his pigeon hole when I got back to Nuuk. He assigned me to prisoner escort to get me out of the city, to keep me away from the missing persons desk. And now, thanks to his scheming, I was working a missing persons case. But where it might lead, was anyone's guess. I needed to collect my thoughts.

I slipped out of the dining room and into the hotel reception. Juuliu's power screwdriver was back on Niinu's desk, and two batteries were plugged in and charging. I paused to listen for the door banging in the wind, nodding when I heard it. Juuliu had yet to screw the door shut, and I wondered if I should have another look in the cellar, only to realise that I still couldn't get inside the inner room, unless there was another door leading down to it, perhaps from some other room in the hotel. I tried to picture the location of the cellar, closing my eyes, and turning on the spot on the reception carpet, as I tried to orientate myself. Spatial relations wasn't one of my strong points, but if I concentrated I could picture the location of the cellar beneath me, and the inner room a little forward and to the right. I turned, opened my eyes, and looked straight at the kitchen door, pinched between the dining room to the left and the study to the right.

The kitchen had a narrow entrance, with a side door into the dining room, and a wall with the outline of a door, now filled-in, that confirmed my earlier thought that the study was once a pantry. The kitchen itself opened up into a large working area with a walk-in freezer on my left. By my own reckoning, the freezer was directly above the room in the cellar. I reached for the handle, only to jump at the sound of someone saying my name.

"It is Petra, isn't it, Honey?" Jordan asked as she stepped into the kitchen.

"Yes," I said.

I let go of the door handle, noting that the key was broken in the lock, and that there were two D rings, one on the door and one on the frame, where I might have expected to see a clasp.

"I just wondered if you were ready for me?" Jordan looked at her watch. "Only, it's getting late, and it looks like everyone wants to stay up until we're done, and, well, I just wanted to move things along a bit. If that's all right with you?"

"It's fine," I said, shelving my thoughts of what might be inside the freezer, and, more importantly, what might be below it. "Shall we sit in the study?"

"Yes," she said. "I'll follow you."

15

There was something different about Jordan. Gone was the nervous ring twisting I noticed the first time she came into the study. She was stronger now, and I wondered if it had anything to do with Bradley Washington, and Mosaic's implications regarding his behaviour. The Jordan I sat next to at dinner had returned, and she smiled as I sat down opposite her.

"What do you want to know, honey?"

Not for the first time, I felt the need to remind Jordan – to remind all of them – that this was not my idea, that I wasn't a detective, and that I was just stranded on the island, waiting for a break in the weather before returning to Nuuk.

But I didn't say anything.

I was too curious to stop now.

"How about I tell you about myself? How's that, honey?"

Jordan didn't wait for me to answer. She made herself comfortable in the chair, crossing her long legs before she began. I tried to guess her age as she talked, noting the fine wrinkles around her mouth and the tightness of her skin. I thought she was in her mid to late fifties, and her story confirmed it.

"I wasn't always a dietician," she said. "I started out in entertainment. I was a dancer. You know, like a showgirl?" Jordan uncrossed her legs, lifting one of them high above the desk, making me wonder if I could do the same. "I worked all the shows in Vegas, met so many people, caught so many breaks. But I always knew it was a short-term gig. None of the girls were much older than thirty, not back then anyway. So, right before the summer, back in the 90s, I took my money, borrowed a car – a convertible – and I took a road trip. Just me, a couple hundred dollars, and a tank of gas. So liberating."

I could just see the desert roads that Jordan described, could almost feel the hot wind blowing through my hair, and I thought about Atii, how the two of us should take a road trip, before either of us settled down. America would be perfect, especially as there are no roads between the towns and villages in Greenland.

"And that's when I met Justin."

"In the 90s?" I asked. I felt the pinch of my skin between my eyes as I tried to remember how old Justin was in the photo. He didn't look much older than Niinu.

"Late nineties. Maybe 1999. He was just a kid then, honey. He could have been ten or eleven. He had these big brown eyes." The skin around Jordan's eyes creased as she smiled. "I was wearing my showgirl shorts and he couldn't take his eyes off my legs. Of course, I didn't mind. I was used to people looking. It was my job. Anyway," Jordan said with a sigh. "Justin's father was the real catch. He sold insurance and I told him he could try and sell me insurance if he bought me dinner." Jordan paused at the memory. "That was the funniest thing.

CONSTABLE PETRA JENSEN 1-3

Little Justin spent the whole night staring at me, right up until the time his daddy started talking insurance. Then he switched from me to his dad, as if there was nothing more interesting than talking premiums and percentages. I remember," she said, with another smile, "he took one of his daddy's pens – plucked it right out of his shirt pocket – then started writing figures on a napkin. Even back then, he had a head for figures. Put that together with his looks and as soon he could he started selling insurance. He never went to college."

"Did he sell you insurance?"

"Justin or his daddy?" Jordan laughed. "His daddy didn't sell me anything. I let him pay for my dinner, and I even think he bought me a full tank of gas, but he didn't sell me any insurance."

"But Justin did."

"He sure did, honey. Many years later. You see, his daddy and I swapped addresses; we kept in touch. And that's another funny thing. Justin didn't just have a head for numbers, he had a way about him. I called it his *disaster anticipation*, or something like that. It was like he could predict the most obscure little disasters, then write an insurance policy for that very thing, with the highest rewards at the lowest rates. Then, when the unthinkable happened, we all cashed in."

"Cashed in?"

"I'm sorry, honey. Is it my English? Am I talking too fast?"

"No," I said. "I'm just curious."

"About our insurances? Hell, *everybody's* curious about Justin's insurances. He had to change his company name a few times. He changed the location too." Jordan paused, as if suddenly remembering she was talking to a police officer. "This is a casual talk, detective, isn't it?"

"I'm only a constable," I said.

"That's right. Of course you are. Silly me, I was just thinking about extradition. Like if I told you something here would you be compelled to do something about it?"

"As long as you haven't committed a crime in Greenland," I said. I slipped my hand into my pocket, wondering how Jordan would react if I put my smartphone on the desk. I decided I would just have to make notes once we were finished.

"Crime is such a rotten word," she said. "I don't think what Justin did was *criminal*, although, maybe you should ask Bradley about that, honey. He's the one getting calls from the IRS."

"IRS?"

"Inland Revenue Service. They've been investigating him on and off ever since the fire. Somehow his condos burned down."

"Was it arson?"

"Lightning," Jordan said. "The strangest thing. It was like the finger of God reaching down, touching Bradley's condos on the very day they were finished, and then torching them. All three."

"We don't have lightning in Greenland," I said.

"Never?"

"Maybe once a year, around Nuuk. Sometimes never." I shrugged. "It's the climate. Too dry, I think."

"That's curious."

"Yes," I said. "But Bradley's condos... Did the lightning strike one of them and the fire spread to the others?"

"Oh no, honey. All three of the condos got hit by lightning."

"But lightning strikes are part of a normal insurance. Aren't they?"

"That's right. But Justin wrote an extra clause in the event that all three condos were struck by lightning on the same day. I think they call it *force majeure*, when something extraordinary happens. But lightning isn't extraordinary, so writing a special clause for three strikes on the same day, didn't raise too many eyebrows. He got away with it."

"But if they were all in the same place," I said, as the pinch of skin between my eyes tightened.

"Oh no, honey, Bradley was building condos in three different locations. Lightning was always a possibility, but Justin made it more interesting with the *all in one day* clause. Of course, *that's* what the IRS are so keen to investigate. It raised their eyebrows. That and when they caught him going through Justin's office after his disappearance."

"Bradley was in Justin's office?"

"Back in Lincoln, Missouri, honey. He said he was just helping out and cleaning up, once Justin was legally declared dead. He took Justin's computer, his extra hard drives and all the paper he could find. Justin's dad was dead – car accident. His mother was nowhere to be found, and Bradley was just doing what any friend would do. That's what he said. But you have to wonder what he was looking for."

I nodded, but a lot of what Jordan said passed over my head, as I focused on one word, the location of Justin's office in *Missouri*.

16

Just as Jordan and I were finishing up, Georgina brought Claudia to the study, and I caught a whisper of something that sounded like a reminder, that they had all agreed to do it, and that Claudia should cooperate, if she was capable of that. The three women bunched at the door, as Jordan left, stepping to one side to give Claudia room to enter. I caught Georgina's eye as she waited at the door, but she was focused on Claudia, and as soon as Claudia started to speak, I understood why.

"She told you about the lightning?" she said, hiking a large thumb over her shoulder as Georgina and Jordan retreated to the dining room.

"Yes," I said, as I switched on the recording app on my phone. "Is it okay if I record the interview?"

"Interview?" Claudia shrugged. "Whatever. I've got nothing to hide."

I paused when she said that, curious that people rarely said it unless there *was* something to hide. It didn't mean that they were hiding something big, but often it was enough to make the statement a lie, however small. Claudia stared at me, and I suddenly felt naked without my utility belt, folding nightstick, and pistol. The desk between us was sturdy, but Claudia and I were the same height, and

I didn't doubt that she could easily reach across it. While Hogan might be the loudest of the group, and Bradley the biggest, Claudia was the most intimidating, and I began to appreciate why Jordan was quick to step out of her way, and why Georgina might have apprehensions about leaving Claudia alone with me in the study. I decided on a gentle course of questioning and picked up where Claudia had left off.

"Tell me about the lightning," I said.

"What about it?"

"You mentioned it."

"So?"

"You wanted to know if Jordan had said anything about it."

"Did she?"

I bit my lip as I realised the roles had been reversed, that it was Claudia asking the questions, and I was feeding her short answers in an attempt to get her to talk.

"You're not very good at this, are you?" she said, cracking her knuckles as she waited for me to respond. "But then, you've been trying to tell us all night, you're just a…"

"Constable," I said.

"Not a detective."

"No."

"All right, *Constable*," Claudia said. "Now we've got that cleared up. What do we do next?"

"Do?"

"This is still an interview, right?"

"Yes," I said, although, up to that point, it was one of the more difficult interviews of my career.

"If I'm going to help you find out what happened to Justin…"

"Another one of Hogan's stupid ideas," Claudia said.

"You don't want my help?"

"I didn't say that." Claudia glanced over her shoulder, as if she half-expected someone to be watching and listening. "I promised Georgina I would be helpful. That I wouldn't be so combative."

"Are you?"

"What?"

"Combative?"

She certainly looked *combative*, but there was something else, just a little deeper. I could see it in her eyes. If Tuukula had been there he would have noticed it. He might even have whispered in my ear, or, more likely, asked a cryptic question with a raised eyebrow, while he waited for me to figure it out for myself. I suddenly felt incredibly alone, and vulnerable, and longed for a more familiar face. I started at what felt like phantom palms on my thighs, as if Luui was squirming into my lap, making herself comfortable. It was at once alarming and reassuring, and the presence – whether a figment of my own imagination or a shamanic projection – was enough to give me a boost of confidence.

"What just happened?" Claudia asked.

"When?"

"Just now." She raised a stubby finger and let it drift between us, pointing at my eyes, before letting her hand fall to her thigh. "It's like you were gone for a moment."

"Maybe I was," I said. "It's been a long day."

"And it's getting late."

I let my shoulders sag a little, and then thought once more about Tikaajaat, and how chatty he had been on the flight from Kulusuk to Nuuk. A little caffeine and a few kind words had really opened him up. Claudia, regardless of the tough image she projected, looked like someone who could really use a chat, a chance to talk.

I reached for my smartphone, turned the recording app off, and slipped it into my pocket.

"What are you doing?" she said with a frown creasing her wide forehead.

I stood up, mentally brushing Luui from my lap and sent a silent *thanks* northwards. I gestured at the door, and said, "I'd like a coffee. I think there might be some left in the kitchen."

I didn't wait for Claudia. I just smiled as I walked around the desk and out of the study. I heard the creak of her chair as she stood up and then the heavy tread of her boots as she followed me to the kitchen.

"There's no fresh milk," I said, as I plucked two clean cups from the coffee trolley. "But the UHT milk isn't so bad if it's cold."

"I'll take it straight, no cream," Claudia said, nodding her thanks as I handed her a cup. "I don't know how you cope with life up here." Claudia leaned against the kitchen counter, and I rested against the oven in the centre of the kitchen, sipping my coffee as she talked. "I mean, it's so barren, so cold, and the milk…"

"We get fresh milk in Nuuk," I said.

"How?"

"On a ship from Denmark."

"And how about the cold? Is it always like this?"

I paused for a second to listen for the storm. The wind had died down a little, reducing the bang and thud of the cellar door to a softer slap and crack.

"There are storms in the fall and spring. Then, in summer, if we've had a few days of clear skies with lots of sun, we'll have a day or two of wind." I shrugged. "It's just the way it is."

"But it doesn't rain?"

"In Nuuk? It rains a lot, half the year – at least, that's what it feels like. But up here. I don't know. It's drier, I guess."

"You're not from the island?"

"I grew up in Nuuk," I said. "I'm a city girl."

"I grew up on a farm." Claudia put her cup down and held up her hands. "See? Farmer's hands. As a kid, I learned how to fork hay and wring chicken necks before I started school. And when I got to school, if there was a fight, you can bet I was in it. It got so bad, even when I wasn't fighting, they had my parents come pick me up. I think it made the other parents feel safer."

"You had a temper," I said, recalling a few of my own fights in the schoolyard, and at the Children's Home.

"Still do." Claudia cast a glance at the door, and then said, "You've seen the way they look at me. Like they're scared."

"Why?"

"Why are they scared?" Claudia reached for her cup and poured herself another coffee. There was something new in her eyes when she turned around – a sharp light, burning with a new intensity. "They all told you stuff. I bet they told you about Justin and his insurance scams."

"Scams?"

"Yeah, you know, a *fraud*. Because that's what he was – a real fraud. Sure, he was nice guy, and he was real nice to me. We met in high school. Not many guys had paid me much attention, but Justin was different. He was soft when he wanted to be, when he wasn't distracted."

Claudia looked at the door leading to reception, and I wondered who she expected to walk through it.

"So, I fell for him. He was a bit older, and I just worshipped the ground he walked on. And he knew that. Even I could see that. But I didn't care. And then, later, when he asked me to help him out, I was ready to do anything. I didn't even care about the money, even though he said there would be a lot of it, once things started to pan out."

I had to concentrate as Claudia relaxed into her story, as the words flowed into a softer southern accent. I used to think I was good at English, but some of the words escaped me, until Claudia said something that reminded me of what Jordan had said earlier.

"Jordan said something about *disaster anticipation*," I said.

"She said that?" Claudia laughed.

"She said he was good at it."

"There was nothing to anticipate," Claudia said. "There was nothing magic about those disasters. Justin either knew they were going to happen, or he made sure they happened."

"Like the lightning," I said.

"Yeah, like lightning. I mean, how about that? Sure, lightning can strike more than a few places during a storm, and that's what Justin was counting on. He just waited for a storm, then made sure lightning struck where he wanted it to."

"How did he do that?"

A wry smile curled the corner of Claudia's mouth. "He just asked. That's how."

I listened as Claudia explained how Justin convinced Bradley to hire her to work on his condos, and how she had helped the electrician with the wiring.

"I even did a little myself, when the electrician called in sick one day."

"And the lightning?"

"There was a storm, and there were a couple of strikes. And then a couple more, if you know what I mean?"

I think I did, but Claudia's insight into Justin's ability to anticipate disaster left me wondering.

"Did he ask you to help with other things too?"

"Other scams, you mean?"

"Yes," I said, curious as to how far Claudia was willing to go, how much she was prepared to tell me.

"I liked Justin," she said. "I liked him a lot. He made me feel safe. He made me feel wanted."

"So, when he asked?"

"I said *yes*." Claudia shifted on her feet, pressing a thick thumb to her eye, and catching a tear in the whorls of her skin. "Of course, you could never prove it," she said, sniffing back another tear before looking at me. "At least not directly. All the policies were on file – on his computer and in some banker boxes in the office."

"In Missouri," I said.

"Right."

Claudia paused, as if waiting for me to reveal what I knew about Missouri.

"Jordan said Bradley helped clean out the office."

"Oh yeah. That's *exactly* what he did."

I felt a breath of cold air on my cheek, as if Tuukula was standing beside me. The bigger picture was forming, and I could see it now. Justin with his uncanny ability to write the most unlikely policies with the lowest premiums, and the greatest benefits. Claudia made them happen, allowing everyone else in the group to reap the rewards. But only if someone tidied everything up, sweeping away the trail. Someone like Bradley.

"But," I said, feeling the pinch of my skin above my nose. "Justin was a broker. What about the companies that underwrite the policies? They would have records."

"Justin had a way around that. He worked with insurance companies who were connected to hedge funds – people with more money than sense, sometimes. He rarely used the same company twice and would always have this *what are the odds* kind of smile ready whenever they questioned him about it, right up to the moment they had to pay up."

"And then?"

"He handled the money, took his cut, and then changed his company name."

"What was his cut?"

"He took thirteen percent, sometimes fifteen."

"Is that a lot?"

"Most brokers take two to eight percent on the premiums. But Justin took his cut of the compensation. Thirteen percent of three condos is a lot of money," she said.

"Yes," I said, as another cold breath tickled my cheek.

It was beginning to make sense, how such an unlikely group of people came together. But the bigger question of why they might stay together, especially after Justin's disappearance, still remained unsolved, and I felt the pinch of my frown deepen.

17

I was still reluctant to disturb Simonsen's evening off. Nor did I want to bring in the officer on duty. Until such time as I had hard evidence that a crime had been committed, I was, technically, just an off-duty constable talking with tourists about a missing persons case, that, according to Niinu, was closed nearly two years ago. Simonsen hadn't found Justin Moon's body then, and I had nothing new to add to the case. Justin was going to remain *disappeared* long after the weather cleared, and long after everyone went home.

And yet, two years after his disappearance, his friends and acquaintances came back.

Why?

I tidied away the milk and coffee, lingering by the freezer, if only to look at the handle one more time, before putting the carton of milk in the refrigerator. The location of the walk-in freezer still fit with where I had positioned the inner cellar in my mind, and I was tempted to look inside.

The door opened easily, almost *too* easily, as if it had been broken once, and the seal had never quite been the same. There were shelves lining the three walls, and cardboard boxes of imported vegetables on a table in the middle of the freezer. I wondered what tourists would make of the freezer as it also stored a range of deep-frozen Greenlandic delicacies in various states of preparation. Sea gulls hung upside down like lazy white bats, with hooks tucked beneath string tied around their feet. They had not been plucked. Arctic hare hung beside them, in much the same way. Seal ribs were also hooked and hanging from a rack stretching the width of the freezer room, together with huge slabs of liver-dark meat, which I recognised as fin whale. To the outsider it was undoubtedly a macabre collection of Arctic birds and mammals, but to a local, it was a rich collection of energy-giving meats, apart from the gulls. I had yet to meet anyone who ever really craved a breast of what was often referred to as Greenlandic chicken.

But I wasn't looking for meat and vegetables.

I walked around the table, squeezing between one side and the shelves, knocking the seal ribs, and throwing shadows on the walls as the ribs swayed in front of the naked yellow bulb. The door closed with a soft snick, but I didn't think anything of it, as closer inspection of a tear in the linoleum covering the floor revealed a rectangular piece that could, if I moved the table, be removed. I lifted a corner, holding my breath as I pulled the linoleum flap past a handle cut into a recess of what looked like a trap door.

"Leading down into the cellar," I said. My breath frosted in front of my face, coating the tips of my black hair in brittle white sleeves of ice.

I let the flap fall back onto the floor and walked around the table to the door. I needed help to move the table if I was going to get access to the cellar.

I gripped the door handle, letting go as I felt the metal stick to my warm palms. I tried again, using the sleeve of my shirt as a glove. The handle turned but the door didn't budge. The seal was better than I had thought, and now, despite my Greenlandic genes, the cold was beginning to affect me, and not just with thicker sleeves of ice in my hair, but with a stiffening of the fine hairs on my arms, ice coating my eyelashes, and a tightening of my skin.

I was stuck inside the freezer.

I gave up on the door and tried my phone, cursing the lack of signal, before chiding myself for even thinking that I would be able to get one. The walls of the freezer room were metal, everything was insulated, and, in a horrible moment, I wondered if it would be soundproofed too.

Still clutching my phone in one hand, I bunched my hands into fists and drummed the door, yelling for help. The thumps and echoes rippled around the walls, and the vibration set more ribs twisting in the light. The dead gulls spun from their hooked feet, beaks clacking against cold metal each time they hit the wall. The hares thumped their frozen flanks against each other, and, as I misted the chill air with breathy shouts, the bulb dulled with puckered patterns of ice.

I stopped banging, forcing myself to stay calm, and take several deep, cold breaths, as I considered my options and planned my next move.

It was still cold outside the hotel, but no colder than the inside of the freezer. It might even be warmer below the freezer. I looked at the table, clenching my jaw as my teeth started to clatter. If I had found help, I would have stacked the boxes to one side, then moved the table out of the freezer and into the kitchen.

But I didn't have help. Nor did I have my jacket, or even my utility belt. I had no tools. Only a useless smartphone, and a pair of regulation boots.

"Training is over, Jensen."

Of course, of all the voices I could channel in that moment, of all the help and assistance I might want, it had to be Sergeant Duneq who spurred me into action. The thought of him shaking his head and wobbling his jowls at the news of me being found dead in a hotel freezer, together with a host of *I told you so* comments that he was so very good at, gave me the strength to brace myself against the door, and kick at the table, again and again until it rocked and then crashed onto the floor. I reached for the flap of linoleum, tearing it off the floor, only to gasp, breathless, as the trapdoor refused to budge, sealing my fate.

18

I tucked a piece of cardboard under my bottom and hugged my knees to my chest. My teeth chattered until I clamped my chin between my knees, convincing myself that I wasn't giving up, I was just regrouping, or *rethinking*. I was doing *something*, or rather I thought I had better *start* doing something, as freezing to death in a walk-in freezer just wasn't how I wanted my life to end. Once the thought was out there, it felt logical to explore the alternatives. Death was always close at hand in Greenland. Of course, there were plenty of ways to die in other countries, but the difference in Greenland was that just hurting oneself could mean death when help was often so very far away. The weather played its part too, helping or hindering the help in ever reaching the victim.

Victim.

That's what I was or was in danger of becoming.

Being a victim should have come naturally to me. I lost my parents before I could remember. I grew up with strangers in a Children's Home. I never learned the language of my country and struggled with my identity because of it. I had every chance to *be* the victim, but somehow, I had always resisted it. Somehow, I had fought back. And I damned well wasn't going to give up twenty-three years of fighting to be me, just to die in a hotel freezer.

I pushed myself to my feet, clamped my jaw shut, and strode to the door.

The first few thumps with my fists were pathetic, as the base of my palm was too soft to make much more than a soft thud that echoed inside the freezer rather than out into the kitchen. I tried punching instead, yelling with each crunch of my knuckles, slamming them harder and harder, screaming away the pain and the cold, oblivious of what, if anything was happening outside the freezer, until, finally, I heard someone shouting for me to stop from the other side of the door.

"You have to stop. The door is locked. I'm trying to open it."

I stopped, letting my fists fall to my sides, ignoring the throbbing in my knuckles as I wondered how the door could be locked. There was no lock. The key had been broken off inside it, and the clasp ripped away, leaving just two metal rings with nothing to connect them.

"Petra," Niinu said, as she opened the door.

I stepped into the kitchen, feeling the warm, dry air wash over me, as Niinu pulled me into her arms. I shivered in her grip, until we sank to the floor and I pressed my arms around her, partly for warmth, drawing her heat into my body, but also to stop the shaking – mine *and* hers.

"He promised it would never happen again," Niinu said.

I heard the words but struggled to say anything.

I was too cold, and my throat stung from shouting and screaming.

"He promised."

I stopped shaking long before Niinu did. When I felt her hot tears running down my neck, I managed to lift my head and find my voice.

"Who promised?" I said, after clearing my throat.

"*Ataata*," she said. "He was supposed to fix it, so it could never happen again."

"Fix what?"

"The door." Niinu lifted her head, and I felt her hands slide off my back as she relaxed her grip. "He broke the key in the lock. He removed the clasp. But still," she said, showing me the tongs, she held in her hand. "Still it could be locked."

"It was locked?"

"*Aap*. Someone stuffed these into the rings."

I took the slim tongs from Niinu's hand, stifling a laugh as I realised I might have died because of a kitchen utensil.

"For olives," Niinu said. "When we have a salad bar."

"Someone locked me in the freezer," I said, clenching my bloody fist around the tongs.

"*Aap*."

"And its happened before?"

Niinu looked into my eyes for a moment, then dipped her head, turning away. I wanted to ask her about it but struggled to think further than the fact that someone had deliberately shut me inside the freezer. The list of suspects was short. But I wanted to finish the interviews before I confronted any of them.

"Niinu," I said. "Let's pretend this didn't happen."

"What?"

"I don't want you to say anything."

"Why?"

"Because now I want to finish this. I want to find out what happened to Justin, but it's personal now." I pressed the tongs into Niinu's hand, and then reached up to the counter to pull myself onto my feet. "But I'll need your help," I said. "And one more thing."

Niinu waited as I brushed the last of the frost from my hair.

"I'd like to borrow your fleece."

Niinu stood up and removed her jacket. She watched as I pulled it on and zipped it to my chin. The shivering had slowed and I felt almost warm again. I patted the pockets to make sure there wasn't anything inside them. The last thing I wanted to do was crumple another of Niinu's personal letters. That's when I remembered *Missouri*.

"I'm sorry, Niinu," I said. "But there is one more thing you can help me with."

Niinu raised her eyebrows, the silent Greenlandic *yes*.

"I'm going to talk to Georgina. But I'd like to talk to you afterwards. Before you go home."

Niinu nodded and excused herself. I waited as she walked out of the kitchen, and then checked my phone. It was time to call Simonsen.

19

Uummannaq's chief of police held a grand title with plenty of responsibility concentrated in a small population spread out over seven settlements, with varying degrees of accessibility. To disturb him on a night off was, as I discovered, like goading dragons, or at least, that's what it felt like. The fact that it was late, and the storm was still raging, only added to Simonsen's abrasive manner as he responded to my call for help. We agreed that he would come to the hotel in one hour.

"Just don't do anything stupid, Constable," he said.

"I'll try not to."

Simonsen's concern was carefully wrapped inside a mouthful of grit, but it made me smile – my first since Niinu rescued me from the freezer.

I picked up my phone charger from my room before I went looking for Georgina, setting it to charge and placing it on the desk between us as I started the interview.

"Are you all right?" she asked. "You look a bit peaky?"

I nodded that I was fine, but my cheeks were flushed and probably quite rosy. I said nothing about the freezer, preferring to keep the incident quiet until Simonsen arrived.

CONSTABLE PETRA JENSEN 1-3

"What do you want to know, Detective?"

I was too tired to correct her and jumped right in with a more direct line of questioning than I had taken with her travelling companions – I no longer thought of them as friends.

"What happened the night Justin disappeared?"

"You mean the very night?"

"Yes."

"It's such a long time ago," Georgina said. "I'm not sure I can remember all the details."

I checked that the app on my smartphone was recording, and then leaned back in my chair as Georgina recalled the last night of her previous visit to Greenland.

"We ate together," she said. "We all sat at the same table. Of course, Claudia sat next to Justin, again. She was besotted with him; we all knew it. But Justin had eyes for someone else that night." Georgina's lips creased at the memory, and I was tempted to ask who, but she continued before I could say anything. "Then we agreed to have a Greenlandic coffee. You know, the one with all the spirits and liqueurs to represent the land, and the sea, and the…"

My thoughts drifted as she described the drink invented for tourists. I had never enjoyed it, and could rarely justify the cost of it, but the tourists seem to get a kick out of it. Instead, I wondered who might have caught Justin's attention, and I realised I had known ever since I found Niinu's letter in her jacket pocket.

"And then I saw Justin leave the hotel, to go for a walk."

"Sorry," I said, as I jolted back into Georgina's recollection of the events leading up to Justin's disappearance. "He went for a walk?"

"Yes."

"But there was a storm," I said. "Everyone agrees on that."

"It was pretty wild," Georgina said. "But I guess Justin wanted to feel the power of nature, if you know what I mean? He could be like that at times. It was part of his charm."

A shadow of something flickered across Georgina's eyes, and I wondered just how fond her recollections of Justin were.

"And did you see him return?"

"You mean did I see him come back to the hotel? No," she said. "I never saw him again." Georgina shifted in her seat, scratching at a stain she noticed on her trousers. It felt like a diversion, as if she was considering what to say next. She tutted at the stain, then clasped her hands in her lap, lifting her head to look at me. "I don't know what Claudia told you," she said. "But perhaps you could ask her where she was that evening. Everyone knew she had a crush on Justin. And he just played her along. She would do anything for him. *Anything.* If that isn't enough to make one wonder, then I don't know what is."

"Wonder about what?"

"Her motives, of course."

Georgina tilted her head slightly to one side, as if she was dealing with a small child. She was different to how she had been on the plane when I first met her, and even at dinner. Something had changed, and it made me wonder if she knew anything about the freezer, and how I came to be locked inside it.

"You think Claudia did something to Justin?"

"I think she had every reason to. Especially after he was so taken with the young Greenlander in reception."

"Niinu?"

Georgina nodded. "It wasn't the first time they had met. They knew each other from Justin's previous visits to Greenland. He had an adventurous streak, something he applied to his business, and in his free time. Of course, with all the money he was making, he could afford to come to places like Greenland. And, obviously, he liked it here. So much so he persuaded us to come with him. He called it *a trip of a lifetime*, because, as you know, it's so expensive to come here."

"And you all decided to come on this trip together?"

"Yes."

"As friends?"

Georgina nibbled at her lip as she thought, and then said, "You think we're friends?"

"No," I said.

"But you called us *friends*."

"I think you're connected," I said. "I think Justin connects you."

"Of course, he does. We're all in his pocket, even now."

"Because of the insurances?"

"Yes." Georgina sneered as she spat the word from her mouth. "Those damned things, and that bloody man." She shifted in her seat, fidgeting with an energy that seemed to come from somewhere deep inside her. "You know, he insured anything for anyone."

"I know he insured the fur on your dog," I said.

"Hogan told you that, did he?"

"Yes."

Georgina's cheeks flushed with a heat to match the fire burning in her eyes.

"He probably told you that Portland shed his fur, that he had a disease. It wasn't the mange, if that's what you're thinking. It was hereditary, something the breeder should have told me. The compensation I got for handfuls of fur, was nothing to what I could have got for the chance to put Portland out to stud. His pedigree was impeccable, or it should have been, if she hadn't conned me. I would have been better off with the other insurance Justin wrote."

"For Portland?" I asked, my brow pinching as I tried to keep up.

"What?"

"You said something about another insurance?"

"Did I?" Georgina said. She turned her attention back to the stain on her trousers, then stood up suddenly, flicking her finger at my smartphone. "You have everything you need, Detective. I saw Justin leave. No one saw him come back. He probably shivered to death on his walk, or maybe fell through the ice. It would be just like Justin to stride out onto the sea ice in a storm. Or maybe someone pushed him?" Georgina shrugged. "But what do I know? I wasn't in love with him."

CONSTABLE PETRA JENSEN 1-3

She turned, and walked to the door, stopping briefly with one last comment.

"You're right about one thing," she said. "We're not friends. We're just forced to be with one another."

"Because of Justin."

"That's right."

"And now? You're still forced to be with each other?"

"Because Bradley didn't do his job properly. If he had, we wouldn't be here chasing ghosts."

She left before I could ask another question, brushing past Niinu, as she hovered by the door.

"I'm going home soon," Niinu said. "But I'm ready to talk now. If you want to hear what I have to say?"

"Yes," I said. "But not here. Is there somewhere else we could go?"

Niinu nodded, and then pointed back towards reception. "We can go to the office," she said. "It's quieter there."

20

Niinu opened the office door and pointed at the tiny sofa pressed against the wall opposite the desk. She pulled a bundle of envelopes out of a drawer and placed them on the desk, before pulling one more out of the back pocket of her jeans. The envelopes were all the same size, with the same handwritten addresses. I guessed that, on closer inspection, the return address would be Lincoln, Missouri.

"From Justin to Justin," Niinu said, pressing the envelope in her hand to her nose. "This one was to me," she said, after a short sniff of the envelope.

"He wrote to you?"

"After his very first visit." Niinu looked at the empty chair by the desk, then chose to sit on the floor, curling her knees to her chest, and clutching the envelope in her hand as she rocked, gently, back and forth as she began her story. "He came on one of the adventure cruise ships one summer. I was selling beads and *Tupilaq* at a store on the grass by the harbour. Justin bought a few things, then came back to buy some more. He wasn't your typical tourist; he was too young. Most of them are old, with money. So, he was different, and exciting." She laughed and a light sparked in her eyes. "He wore one of those life vests – the tube kind that inflate if you fall in the water. The cruise ships make people wear them, even on land. Justin took his off and gave it to one of the passengers. I got worried when the tourists headed back to the boat. The ship's horn blew, and he just stayed there, chatting with me, as his ship sailed away."

"He missed his boat," I said.

"*Aap*," Niinu said. "He missed it for me." The light in her eyes shone brighter as the first tears began to slip down her cheeks. "He said I was more fun than a boat full of old people. I said he was crazy, and he said we could be crazy together." Niinu wiped her cheeks with her hand, pausing to dry a stray tear that landed on the envelope. "He stayed for two weeks, sometimes at the hotel, and then at my house, when *ataata* went fishing. He never promised anything, but he said he would be back. He came back twice, before the third and last time."

Niinu dipped her head to her knees and I got up from the sofa to join her on the floor.

"Tell me what happened," I said, softly, as I wrapped my arm around her shoulders.

"He said they were his business partners," she said, lifting her head and sniffing back another round of tears. "He didn't call them friends. He said they made money together. And he always seemed to have money, I just never thought to ask where it came from." She paused to look at the bundle of envelopes on the desk. "He started sending them a few times a year after we met. He asked me if I would hold onto them. He said they had something to do with insurance, and that was his business. But I got confused when he said they were *insurance*.

He said it was important that I keep them safe. My English is good but it's difficult when the words have two different meanings."

I knew exactly what she meant, and told her so, brushing another tear from her cheek with my thumb. "Keep going," I said, hoping that she would.

Niinu took a breath and nodded. "When I found you in the freezer, I got so scared. I knew I had to tell you. But we've told no one. Not even the police." Niinu paused for another breath, the hollow kind that are breathy with no benefits. "Justin never left Uummannaq," she said. "He's still here."

"Here?"

"In the hotel," she said, and then, "*Ataata* said he would fix the freezer door. He said it would never happen again. He broke the key in the lock. He removed the clasp. After what happened; he had to do it."

"Juuliu helped you?"

"*Aap*," Niinu said. "But he said we couldn't tell anyone. And I didn't. But then seeing you in the freezer, knowing that you might have died if I didn't find you." Niinu turned within my arms to take my hand, pressing Justin's letter between us. "The people who came with him, wanted to be with him all the time. If they saw him talking to one of the group the others joined them, as if they didn't want him to be alone with anyone. As if they didn't trust him. So, when they were here, we couldn't be together, and I wanted to be with him, like we had been the other times. But they were always there. They never let us be alone."

"So, you made a plan to meet him?" I said,

thinking it was what I would have done, before reminding myself that, probably, Atii would have made the plan and I would have done what she told me to.

"*Aap*," Niinu said. "He told them he was going for a walk. But there was a storm. And no one wanted to go outside. It was too cold. But one of them waited in the armchair in reception."

"Who?"

"Jordan, I think. It was like they were keeping an eye on him and wanted to know when he came back. I think they all agreed that she should wait."

"But he wasn't coming back that way, was he?"

"*Naamik*," Niinu said, with a shake of her head. "I told him there was another way into the hotel, that he could get back in with no one seeing him."

"How?"

"Through the cellar, and then through the trapdoor…"

"Into the freezer."

"*Aap*." Niinu gripped my hand tighter as her body started to shake. "He was supposed to come up through the trapdoor and out of the freezer, into the kitchen."

"But the door was locked," I said.

"And the key was missing." Niinu's long nails pinched my skin. "I couldn't open it and couldn't break it. I told Justin to go back down the trapdoor before he froze."

"But he couldn't."

Niinu shook her head. "The trapdoor was bolted from below." She bit her bottom lip until it turned white, and I brushed another stream of tears from her cheeks. "He was inside, and I heard him, just like I heard you, banging and kicking and shouting. I called *ataata*, but he never answered. Then I tried to get help, but there was no one around. All his friends were gone, even the woman sitting in the armchair."

"Jordan?"

"*Aap*, I think so. She was gone. The chair was empty."

"And Justin?"

I shouldn't have asked. I knew what he would have felt, as the cold seared his skin, puckered his lips, and frosted the hairs on his body, before sinking deep into his bones, slowing his body, chilling his core.

"He stopped shouting," Niinu said. "I couldn't help him."

"But your father came?" I said, after a moment's pause.

Niinu nodded, unable to speak.

I spoke for her.

"He broke into the freezer."

"*Aap*."

"But Justin was dead."

Niinu sniffed and then held her breath. She exhaled with ragged nods of her head. Then, after another pause, she found the strength to continue, her voice clearer with each step of her confession.

"*Ataata* went out of the hotel and into the cellar. He threw back the bolt and then we carried Justin through the trapdoor. There are coffins down there."

"I've seen them," I said.

"They were empty," Niinu said. "They used to

be the carpenter's but were never used. Until we put Justin inside one of them."

"You didn't tell anyone?"

"I thought I killed him." Niinu pressed her hand to her mouth, whispering through her fingers. "I *did* kill him. I told him to go outside, to sneak back into the kitchen. He died in the freezer."

"No, Niinu," I said. "It wasn't you. You didn't throw the bolt on the trapdoor. Somebody else did. Just like they locked the freezer."

"Why? Why would they do that?"

I took a moment before answering, looking once more at the envelopes on the desk, wondering if the answer was inside them.

Niinu crumpled her envelope to her face, and I teased it from her hands, flattening it on my thigh, before placing it in her lap. We both turned our heads as someone wearing heavy boots clumped along the short corridor to the office. Niinu held her breath as they knocked on the door, nodding when I asked if she was ready.

"Come in," I said, as I slid across the floor to make room for the door to open.

Simonsen looked into the room and then down at the two of us on the floor. He frowned, and then moved towards the sofa.

"Can I sit down?" he asked.

Niinu nodded, her hand still clasped to her mouth. I waited until Simonsen sat down, and then quietly closed the door.

"Niinu," I said. "I think I know what happened next. Can I tell the Chief?"

"*Aap*," she said, before hugging her knees even

tighter to her chest.

Simonsen looked at me, and I picked up the story where Niinu had stopped.

"About two years ago," I said, looking at Simonsen. "You were involved in a search for Justin Moon."

"That's right," Simonsen said, with a glance at Niinu. "We never found him."

"That's because he's in the hotel cellar…"

"What?"

"In one of the carpenter's coffins."

"What the hell?"

"Chief," I said, as Niinu started to shake. "Just listen a minute. It's not what you think."

"We searched for that man. Couldn't find him. We declared him missing, and then dead, when people said they might have seen a tourist walk out onto the ice."

"What people? Not one of the people he was travelling with?"

"Them?" Simonsen shook his head. "They all left on the first helicopter." He looked at Niinu again, and said, "He's in the cellar?"

"*Aap.*"

"In a coffin?"

"He was dead," she said.

"He froze to death," I said. "In the same way I was going to, if Niinu hadn't found me."

"Okay," Simonsen said. "One of you has to slow down, and the other has to start talking, because I have no idea what's going on right now."

Simonsen paused as the door opened and Juuliu walked into the room.

"Chief?" Juuliu said. "Is everything all right?"

"You tell me, Juuliu. It seems there's a body in your basement, and you never told me about it."

"It's okay, *ataata*," Niinu said. "I told her," she said, pointing at me. "But we have to tell the Chief."

"Tell him everything," I said, as I reached for the envelopes on the desk.

"And while they do that," Simonsen said. "Where will you be?"

"In the study, doing my last interview."

"With whom?"

"Justin Moon," I said.

21

Justin was an insurance broker and his letters were his insurance. I understood that as I opened the first envelope, teasing out a folded piece of American A4 paper, slightly wider and shorter than the European equivalent. Justin had stuffed as many copies of his policies as he could into each envelope, and I spread the contents of each on the desk in front of me. The wind continued to blow, but I didn't hear it. The kitchen door creaked as someone went in and then again when they went out, but I ignored it. In front of me, in varied shades of dark grey to black ink, was a map of straight roads, bends, curves, and intersections, linking each of the people in Justin's special collection of clients. Judging from the specificity of the policies, and the degree of disaster anticipation, cleverly concealed in descriptions of the mundane, from run-of-the-mill to freak-of-nature events, the group Justin had assembled were inseparable, bound by overlapping policies, the compensation from which benefited all of them, albeit not directly, and not without some pain or misfortune.

I opened another envelope and began to see a pattern, in which one month one person benefitted, only for another to profit from that same person's misfortune in the next. What started out as relatively straightforward policies counting on the unthinkable, became calculating claims capitalising on the improbable.

I sorted the claims into piles starting with Hogan.

Hogan's wristwatch seemed to be the most practical and beneficial of the policies, saving him money each time the winder in his watch broke. But when I read the policy covering the use of faulty motors for the drills in his dental practice, the potential compensation was so good, I wondered if it was worth his while to buy better equipment.

Mosaic must have known about Hogan's dodgy drills. Why else would he have Justin write a policy that not only insured his smile, but specifically insured him against dental injury?

But Mosaic insured more than his teeth. I felt the pinch of my frown as I read and then reread his policy ensuring he was compensated in the event that his dietician ever received bad press, so bad it negatively impacted her business. Which made me wonder, how perfectly positioned Mosaic was to influence the rise or demise of his dietician, via his influential lifestyle show on *YouTube*.

Jordan seemed equally interested in bad press, with policies that insured her income against failing popularity, allowing her to explore a side interest in show dogs, Afghan Hounds in particular. But while Georgina insured herself against loss of income from Portland's hereditary mange, turning the world's most glamorous dog into a stubbly chicken – as noted in the margins of Justin's letters – Jordan insured Georgina's dogs in the event of their death.

Again, the specificity was interesting. Georgina had life insurance for her beloved Afghans, but Jordan's insurance of the same dogs covered vehicular death only.

Claudia's car was insured in the same way as Hogan's watch, with one part in particular receiving particular attention in her policy: the bumper. A quick cross-reference of the three women's claims revealed that Claudia replaced her bumper with the same frequency as Georgina's dogs died, the ones suffering from mange.

I leaned back in my chair to take a break. I could feel the pinch of my frown as I considered just how coordinated everything was, as if everybody knew everybody else's business, and policies. Why else would strangers, from different parts of the United States – spread across the whole of America, as far as I could see – have anything to do with each other. Mosaic had to know about Hogan's drills, and the three women must have known about the dogs, the bumpers, and the mange. I spared a thought for Georgina, only to purge any sympathy I might have had when I realised, she was just as calculating as everyone else. She couldn't put her dogs out to stud, if they had inferior genes.

And then there was Bradley and his condos, the ones Claudia worked on, in her capacity as amateur electrician. Judging by the letters, and the details of the policies, it seemed to be the point at which Justin's disaster anticipation faltered into the disastrous. Bradley stood to lose the most, which made it most important that his claim was successful. Justin must have convinced him it would be, and then brought Claudia in to make the improbable possible.

And that was his undoing.

Thicker envelopes with more letters revealed claims investigations, and investigations into Justin's business, and the business of all his associates. Claudia had said they were scams, but Justin's prediction of lightning striking not twice but three times in three different locations on one man's property, drew too much attention.

"And that's why he chose Greenland," I said, as another piece of the puzzle fell into place.

Not quite Europe and not quite America, Greenland was modern enough to be comfortable, but remote enough to disappear. But I don't think Justin chose to disappear permanently, just long enough to weather the storm of fraudulent claims and scams swirling around him and his associates in America.

"So, he brought them here," I said to myself, as I leaned forward to return to the letters. "To make plans to cover their tracks."

I looked up at a knock on the door, nodding as Simonsen stepped into the study.

"You were talking to yourself, Constable."

"Yes," I said.

"Find anything interesting?" Simonsen nodded at the letters spread out on the desk.

"Yes. Lots."

"And any idea who might have locked you in the freezer?"

"Yes," I said. "Some."

"All right," Simonsen said. "You can tell me in

a minute, but first we have to go down into the cellar."

Niinu pressed her jacket into my hands as I left the study. I left Justin's letters on the table, and she locked the door behind me.

"Are you all right?" I asked.

"I'm okay," she said, with a glance at Simonsen. "There are some things we have to work out."

"We'll sort it out," Simonsen said. He tugged at the collar of his jacket, then zipped it all the way above his chin. He nodded at Juuliu, as the janitor stuffed both batteries for the power screwdriver into his pockets, before leading the way into the storm. "Danielsen is on his way," Simonsen said to Niinu. "Wait for him in the office."

I reached out to hug Niinu, and then followed the Chief and Niinu's father into the last breathy gusts of the storm.

The twists and tiny tornadoes of spinning snow had settled into soft powdery plumes, dusting our boots and the cuffs of our trousers. The temperature had dropped, draining the storm's energy, dragging it down to the granite, quashing it between the exposed rocks.

The square cellar door moved listlessly, as if it too was tired of flapping. Juuliu pushed it to one side, then climbed into the cellar. I heard him slap one of the batteries into the screwdriver and begin removing the screws from one of the plywood panels, as I helped Simonsen negotiate the square door.

Once inside, Simonsen tugged the flashlight from his belt and clicked it on, just as Juuliu slid one of the panels to one side. We all blinked in the light of the yellow bulb, before following Juuliu inside the inner cellar.

"I took one of the coffins," he said, pointing at a single coffin clamped between thick granite fingers. "Do you want me to open it?"

"I think you know the answer to that," Simonsen said.

Juuliu nodded and got to work on the lid, as Simonsen turned the beam of his flashlight upwards, revealing the bolt holding the trapdoor in place. He talked as Juuliu worked on the coffin.

"Justin Moon froze to death in the freezer, and then Juuliu lowered his body down here. That's right, isn't it?" Simonsen waited for Juuliu to nod, and then continued. "So, they pulled one of the coffins up here, put Justin in it, and then sealed it off with plywood."

"Making Justin disappear," I said.

Simonsen nodded. "Right now, about the only thing I could get angry about, is the fact that they wasted police time and resources with the search. But, given the situation…"

"It was the best thing they could do."

"And Justin is listed as missing, presumed dead."

Simonsen paused as Juuliu slid the lid off the coffin. No one spoke for what felt like a minute. The chill of winter had, thankfully, purged Justin's corpse of its death smell, but the hot summer had not been kind. I took a moment more, then nodded for Juuliu to replace the lid.

"And now he's dead," Simonsen said. "Confirmed."

22

We gathered in the dining room, with Justin's accomplices – now upgraded from *travelling companions* – sitting around two tables in the centre of the room, while Niinu and her father sat at the table by the window, the one I should have taken before agreeing to dining with the Americans. Simonsen leaned against the wall by the door, thumbs tucked into his utility belt in a comfortably cowboy manner. The two men sitting at the back of the room, next to the kitchen door, were strangers, although I presumed the young constable, perhaps a year or two older than me, was Danielsen. I didn't recognise the Greenlander sitting beside him.

"That's Iinta," Simonsen said, catching my arm before I addressed the group. "You're taking him back to Nuuk."

"Why is he here?"

Simonsen shrugged. "The cells are empty at the moment, and he's bored. I thought a night out would do him good. Besides, he promised to behave himself."

"Okay," I said, biting my lip for want of anything better to say.

"Are we ready, detective?" Hogan said, drumming his fingers on the table.

"*Constable*," I said, forcing a smile on my lips.

"Just like Constable Danielsen, over there, in the corner." Danielsen waved as I pointed at him. "And that's the Chief of Police, Simonsen, standing by the door."

"Chief of Police," Hogan said, and laughed. "What's the name of this place again? Amity Island?"

Simonsen laughed and said something about a film called *Jaws*, and then stepped to one side as Bradley entered the dining room. No one said a word as Bradley walked to the middle of the room. He reached out to take my hand.

"Thank you," he said. "I was out of line, and I was cold. You saved me, Constable."

"You're welcome," I said. I wanted to add that I knew exactly how he felt, but until I felt confident I knew who had slipped the tongs into the freezer door, I preferred not to say anything at all. I waited until Bradley found a seat, before reconstructing the last hours of Justin Moon's life.

All eyes were on me with the occasional glance at Niinu until I reached the part about the coffin, and the fact that Justin's body was in the hotel cellar. At that point heads began to swivel.

"You mean right this minute?" Georgina said. "He's there right now? We can see him?"

"One of you has already tried to."

"What?"

"Bradley," I said, pausing as the group turned their heads and stared at him. "When you followed me into the cellar, you said the sawdust in the snow was fresh."

"That's right."

"And Juuliu's batteries for his screwdriver were empty."

"I don't follow this," Hogan said. "You're saying one of us knew Justin was in the cellar?"

"I'm saying, someone wanted to have a look and see. The same person who knew there was a trapdoor leading into the freezer."

"Who the hell builds a hotel with a trapdoor into a freezer anyway?" Hogan said. "I mean, come on. Bradley? What do you think?"

"The hotel expanded some years ago," I said, with a nod to Juuliu. "I've already told you about the carpenter's house. Before they built a walk-in freezer on top of it, the trapdoor led down to the carpenter's cellar."

"Where the coffins are," Mosaic said.

"Yes," I said. "Exactly. But one of you knew about that, and when you all decided to come back to find out what happened to Justin, that person knew to look underneath the hotel, because they'd been there before."

"What are you saying?" Georgina asked. "Are you accusing one of us of killing Justin?"

"She didn't say that," Hogan said.

"No?" Georgina rounded on Hogan, and said, "She just implied that one of us knew there was a trapdoor down there, and that they went looking for Justin. She's implying that the same person must have been there before."

"And when Niinu told Justin how he could sneak back into the hotel," I said.

"Somebody followed him and locked the trapdoor," Simonsen said in rusty but passable

English, as he took a step away from the wall. "Which makes it murder."

"You can't prove that," Georgina said. She turned to the others. "They can't prove it."

Everyone else stayed quiet, choosing to look at their feet, or at the walls, but not at each, and not at Simonsen or me. All apart from Claudia. She looked straight at me, and, as I opened my mouth to speak, she nodded with what felt like reluctant encouragement.

"Of everyone in the group, you miss him the most," I said, looking at Claudia. "Don't you?"

She nodded.

"You knew about the cellar."

Another nod.

"And you know how to use a power screwdriver."

"It's not difficult," Hogan said. Jordan shushed him.

"So, when you came back," I said. "You went down to the cellar, just as soon as you'd checked in."

"Yes," she said.

"Because that was the last place you had seen Justin."

"Yes."

"Claudia?" Jordan said. "You locked Justin inside the freezer?"

Claudia shrank on her chair, slumping against the backrest as the energy drained out of her, along with her confession. She had yet to admit to anything, but that didn't stop the others from speculating, accusing, and assuming the moral high ground. I felt it was time to bring them all down to the same level, for Claudia's sake, for Justin's and for Niinu's. I looked over to the table where Niinu sat by the window. Niinu reached under the table and pulled out a cardboard box full of Justin's envelopes. Bradley was the first to see it, and he stiffened in his seat. One by one, the others stopped talking.

"You asked me to investigate," I said, taking the box from Niinu. "But I think what you really wanted, was help in finding these."

"And what are they?" Hogan asked.

"Insurance."

"What?"

"These are Justin's copies of all the policies he ever wrote. The ones Bradley was looking for when he cleared out Justin's office."

"I thought you got everything," Georgina whispered.

"No, *George*," Bradley said. "You know I didn't. Why the hell else would we come back here?"

"These letters," I said, "link all of you to Justin. The policies show how each of you used each other to make you and Justin some money. He brought you together, not as friends, but to use you. And then, when he said he was coming to Greenland, that he'd met someone, you didn't like the idea, did you?"

"You're just guessing," Mosaic said.

"Am I? Why would Jordan sit by the door in the reception when Justin went out for a walk? Why would none of you leave him alone, and if he was with one person, you quickly made sure *they* weren't alone. Jordan," I said, turning to look at her. "You said Justin could anticipate disaster."

"Yes?"

"Well, he did. He anticipated this. So, he prepared for it. He sent copies of everything to the hotel, leaving them with Niinu."

"He sent everything here?" Hogan said.

"Yes."

"And all the letters are in that box?"

"All but one," I said.

Niinu stood up and pulled the last envelope from her back pocket. She wiped at the tears on her cheeks, and then took a long breath, holding it as she opened the crumpled envelope. "This was his last letter," she said. Her voice grew stronger as she read, and the pain in her eyes turned into anger, as she stared at the people she thought were Justin's friends. "*...I've done bad things, Niinu, but I'm going to make it right. I'll start again. When I come back to Greenland, it will be for the last time.*" Niinu folded the letter back into the envelope. She pressed it to her chest, and said, "He promised he wouldn't leave, and he didn't. He's still here. He'll never leave."

I waited for Niinu to sit down, and then took a step towards the nearest table. I put down the box, pausing for a second, wondering what I would say next, wondering how to follow Niinu's reading of Justin's last promise – his promise to her.

I was moved, and I took another moment to hold back a tear, dropping my guard for a moment, just long enough for Georgina to push off her seat and make a grab for the box.

She almost made it to the door, only to stop as Iinta met her halfway, peeling back his fist, before slamming it into her nose. Georgina crumpled to the ground, tossing the box above her head, and spilling Justin's envelopes like disembodied wings into the air.

Hogan was the first to reach for the nearest envelope, tearing the paper out of it, quickly followed by Mosaic, Jordan and Bradley. Only Claudia remained seated, resigned to her fate, just a breath away from confessing.

"For God's sake, Iinta," Simonsen said, as he strode across the room towards him. "You promised."

I smiled as Iinta shrugged, accepting the cuffs that Simonsen slapped around his wrists before returning to his seat with a smug, and, in my opinion, thoroughly deserved grin on his face.

Bradley was the first to look up, and the only one to actually look at the papers. The others were too busy tearing them into small pieces.

"These are menus," he said. "Photocopies."

"Yes," I said, as the others slowly realised what was happening. "You could say Justin anticipated this."

"And the real ones?" Bradley asked, as he stood up.

"Are in a safe place," Simonsen said.

I helped Georgina to her feet and into a chair, plucking a serviette from the table to soak up the blood streaming from her nose.

"Constable," Jordan said, as she found a seat.

"Yes?"

"Do you remember what I asked you, during the interview?"

"You wanted to know if we could arrest you, for crimes committed in America."

"That's right," Jordan said. "And you told me that as long as no crimes had been committed in Greenland…"

"Then you were okay," I said.

"Okay. Thank you, honey. I just wanted to be sure."

"I understand," I said. "But there is just one thing." I felt the curl of my lips before I started to speak, but there was nothing I could do to stop the smile from infecting my voice, when I said, "One of you – maybe more than one – locked me in the freezer. That's a crime, if you didn't know. Attempted murder, no less. And it was committed in Greenland." I pointed at the empty cardboard box and the fake letters strewn across the dining room. "Of course, we're going to have to read all these letters – the real ones – if we're going to find out the motive for such a crime. And I think, Chief," I said, looking at Simonsen, "we might need some help with that."

"My English really isn't that good," he said. "I think we'll need some outside help. But until then. The beaches are closed, no one gets on or off the island."

I frowned as Simonsen started to laugh.

"*Jaws*," he said, before ordering everyone to sit down so he and Danielsen could start to process them.

I turned my back on the confusion and walked over to Niinu's table. I found an extra chair and sat down beside her and Juuliu.

"It's not going to be easy," I said. "And there will be lots of questions. But the Chief promised to look after you."

Niinu took my hand and nodded. "*Qujanaq*. Thank you."

"Don't mention it," I said.

I peeled off Niinu's fleece and hung it on the back of the chair, said goodnight, and then walked to the dining room door. Iinta caught my eye and grinned as I passed him.

"Behave," I said, as I walked out of the dining room, leaving Simonsen and Danielsen with the Americans. I had found my third missing person, and I was done for the night.

Epilogue

"It was Claudia," Simonsen said, as he drove Iinta and I to the heliport the next morning. "She put the tongs in the kitchen door. She confessed right after you went to bed. She confessed to everything."

"Just Claudia?"

"No," he said. "She said Georgina made her do it." Simonsen slowed as a gaggle of lively puppies tumbled across the road. "It seems Georgina was a bit of a ring leader. Once Claudia confessed, they all did. All of them pointing fingers at her."

"Which is strange," I said, thinking that it was Bradley who had the most to lose.

"Until you remember the dogs," Simonsen said, beeping the patrol car's horn at the last of the puppies as it flopped down in front of us. "She's a veterinarian who wants to breed her own dogs. They'll never let her do that if they think she intentionally had dogs killed to make a profit."

"It was Jordan who insured Georgina's dogs."

"And Claudia who killed them."

Iinta snorted and I turned to see him shake his head.

"Exactly," Simonsen said, tilting the rear-view mirror so he could look at Iinta.

"Well," I said, as Simonsen parked outside the heliport. "I hope I never get stranded here again."

"Agreed."

Simonsen tapped two cigarettes out of a packet, and nodded for Iinta to join him for a smoke before the helicopter left for the mainland. I took a moment to look at the heart-shaped mountain that gave Uummannaq its name, wondering when or if I would return.

Iinta was far less chatty than Tikaajaat, sipping his coffee as we flew over Disko Bay with little more than a grunt and a shrug of his shoulders by way of conversation. I settled into my seat, content to stare out of the window, as I thought about Niinu and Juuliu, and the promise Simonsen had made to help them. Growing up in Nuuk, though small in comparison to the big cities of Denmark, and even bigger ones further afield, it was easy to forget how intimate life was in the smaller villages and settlements of Greenland. It made police work both varied and interesting, though not without its fair share of tragedy. This time, it was a visitor who had died, but all too often it was a member of the community, someone who would be missed by everyone who knew them, in varying degrees.

I must have been more affected by Justin's disappearance than I thought, as I found myself unusually sympathetic when I thought of Sergeant Duneq, no doubt waiting to berate me back in Nuuk, when he discovered that I had been locked in a freezer, that I had conducted an unofficial *international* investigation, which developed into a murder inquiry, or manslaughter at the very least. It was all in Simonsen's report, and, as my supervisor,

Duneq would have made it his priority to read it. I could just picture his jowls wobbling in anticipation of the tongue-lashing he would give me – as public as possible – the minute I arrived back at the station. But, in my most sympathetic moment, I was ready to thank Duneq for assigning me to prisoner escort, with the added thought that he did have a plan, and that he was working on my transition from newly trained police recruit straight out of the academy, to a competent constable, capable of pulling her weight no matter the assignment.

I held onto that thought as we landed in Ilulissat, the wheels bumping on the newly thawed runway as the month of May warmed up in anticipation of the short spring before summer.

It was Iinta who brought me back to earth, challenging my thoughts about Sergeant Duneq, when he plucked the in-flight magazine from the rack in the airport waiting lounge, and opened it to the article about me and the Greenland Missing Persons desk.

As soon as I saw the headline, followed by the photo, I understood that even if Duneq had a grand plan to expose me to the varied life of a police officer in Greenland, he would not be able to restrain himself once he read the article. I pulled out my smartphone as Iinta read the article, opened my calendar and deleted all the private dates and arrangements I had made for the weekends in the foreseeable future. I had no doubt I would be working the Friday through Sunday evening shifts long into the summer.

"What do you think?" I asked, when Iinta was

finished with the article.

"Who is Sergeant Duneq?" he asked, tapping a dirty nail beside Duneq's name in the article.

"My boss."

"Hmm," he said.

"What does *hmm* mean?"

Iinta said nothing more. He didn't have to. We both knew I was in trouble.

The End

CHRISTOFFER PETERSEN

About the Author

Christoffer Petersen is the author's pen name. He lives in Denmark. Chris started writing stories about Greenland while teaching in Qaanaaq, the largest village in the very north of Greenland – the population peaked at 600 during the two years he lived there. Chris spent a total of seven years in Greenland, teaching in remote communities and at the Police Academy in the capital of Nuuk.

You can find Chris in Denmark or online at

www.christoffer-petersen.com

For exclusive content check out Christoffer Petersen's Patreon page at

www.patreon.com/christofferpetersen

CONSTABLE PETRA JENSEN 1-3

The Greenland Missing Persons series includes

The Boy with the Narwhal Tooth
The Girl with the Raven Tongue
The Shiver in the Arctic
The Fever in the Water
The Winter Trap
The Shaman's Daughter
The Banshee Palace
The Ice Whispers
The Blood Bandit
The Rock Thief
The Glacier Wraith
The Blister at the End of the World
The Boreal Tattoo
The Last Day of Old Magic
The Intrigue in the North
The Polar Bear Screen
The Mammoth Hunt
The Fox that Barked
The Ptarmigan Wing
The Forsaken Fjord
The Empty Cage

and
Crocodile Beat
Glacier Beat
Tundra Beat

Milton Keynes UK
Ingram Content Group UK Ltd.
UKHW011347010823
426147UK00001B/24